THE FAMILY CABIN

A gripping psychological thriller
with a shocking twist

James Caine

ISBN-13: 9798376106280
ISBN-10: 1477123456

Cover design by: Deranged Doctor Design
Library of Congress Control Number: 2018675309
Printed in the United States of America

CHAPTER 1

Amber

My head throbbed with pain. I slowly looked around the room, seeing double. A light above me burned my eyes while I tried to make sense of where I was. The room had cement walls with a matching floor.

I knew I was in a basement but couldn't remember how I got there. I attempted to lift my hands to rub my forehead but felt strong resistance.

My hands were handcuffed behind my back. I began to realize my situation. I leaned forward and nearly fell off the metal chair. The pain in my head was immense, and I winced.

I saw no windows, only a wooden door. A large metal table was against one wall. The room was bare, except for me, the table and the chair.

I let out a sigh of relief when I saw my feet were not tied. I stood up immediately and walked towards the door, but stopped a few feet from it. I looked behind me and found a chain connected to the handcuffs kept me from moving further. I wiggled my hands and watched the chain move. It was connected to a metal hook cemented into the back wall.

A tear formed in my eye as I realized with fear that I had been taken.

"Help!" I cried. "Please! Someone help me!"

I took in a deep breath, trying to calm myself and collect my thoughts. What happened to me? Why couldn't I remember? I attempted to retrace my steps before waking up in this basement, the pain in my head making it more difficult.

I was studying late in the university campus library. I had a midterm exam the next day and wanted to do a cram session. Criminal law. It was a basic course to introduce new law students to the fundamentals we would need to know moving forward.

I had been there most of the day, and night. The library held extended hours during exam times. I sat in a cubicle on the fourth floor, facing a window. It was my favourite spot to study.

I tried not to be superstitious, but I had studied for all my examinations in my undergraduate degree in the same cubicle. The one time I hadn't and pulled an all-nighter in my room the night before, I got a B-, which was truly horrific for me at the time. I promised myself I would always ensure I had a long study session at my fourth-floor cubicle after that.

If I ever got to the library and someone

was sitting in my spot, I would politely ask how long they planned on being there for and would sometimes wait nearby waiting to pounce as soon as they made any signs they were leaving. I couldn't focus right if I wasn't in my cubicle.

It was my special place. My study spot somehow gave me superpowers to remember course materials and ace any test.

The sound of the footsteps above me broke my fantasy and reminded me where I was. I shuddered. They echoed across the ceiling. Whose basement was this? How did I get here?

It had been close to midnight at the library. When I felt comfortable I knew what would be required for my test, I gathered my things to leave. After packing away my laptop, I tossed my oversized University of Calgary sweater on. Although it was a typical cold February day in Alberta, the fourth-floor campus library was always boiling hot.

The footsteps continued above me as I moved around the room as much as the chain allowed. I stood above the table, which was unusually low. I let out an audible gasp as I noticed a dark red stain on one corner.

I looked down. I was still wearing my white campus sweater but saw drops of red marking my shoulder.

My eyes widened as I remembered now. I left the library, waving at the campus police officer who sat at a table near the entrance.

I winced in pain, thinking of my walk to the parking lot where I had parked my beat-up Volkswagen. All I had wanted that night was to grab some McDonald's drive-through, go home, and if my roommate was still up, watch a movie with her.

The university campus was quiet at night, unlike the usual hustle of students during the daytime. The buildings were dark now, with only a few dim lights illuminating the pathways. The grassy lawns were empty.

I remembered feeling uneasy. I thought about turning back to the library. Campus guards had offered to walk me to my car when I studied late. If only I'd taken them up on that offer.

My phone rang loudly, breaking the silence of the night. I jumped and took my cell out of my pants. It was my mom. I rolled my eyes. It was past midnight; what could she want? I knew the answer though and didn't have time to deal with her. I needed sleep. The test was early the next day, and my brain was fried. A late-night argument with my mother was not what I needed. I slipped my phone back into my pocket and could now see the empty parking lot, and my car.

As I neared my vehicle, I took out my keys and unlocked it. That was when I felt the pressure to the back of my head, and then… nothing.

Until I woke up.

I knew I had to find a way out before it was too late. I pulled on the chain, trying to loosen the metal hook from the wall. I screamed for help, hoping someone would hear me. But as the minutes ticked by, I knew I had to come up with a plan on my own. My only hope was to keep my wits about me and find a way to escape from this nightmare.

That's when I heard the footsteps above me move again. They went across the room, and stopped. I took a deep breath realizing the person hadn't stopped moving, but the sound they made had changed.

The thud the person made was soft and muffled, with a rhythmic tapping sound as the heel of the shoe hit each step.

I stared wide-eyed at the wooden door, waiting. I wanted to scream, but my body wouldn't allow me. It was as if someone had taken the batteries out of me and I was stuck in mid-motion, staring at the door.

Even when there was a loud thud on it, I wasn't able to react in any way, besides watch as the door slowly opened. When the person walked into the room, I managed to open my mouth.

He was tall, wearing a red flannel shirt with the sleeves rolled up exposing his thick forearms. He carried a bucket in one hand, placing it on the floor once inside.

I felt my hands behind my back tremble. The

face that stared back at me was one I recognized.

The dead red eyes stared back. Its mouth was open, revealing all of its white, menacing teeth. Its ears were pointed backwards. The mask of the wolf's head that the man wore looked as if it was about to attack me.

"You're awake," the man said, the mask muffling his deep voice. "This is for you." He lowered the bucket to the floor, nudging it with his foot towards me. "Step back," he demanded suddenly. I continued to stare at the menacing mask, not comprehending what he asked. "Step back!" he yelled. I did what was asked this time, moving closer to the chair. "Sit!" his deep voice boomed. I sat on the chair and did not take my eyes off the man with the wolf mask. "Good girl."

The man stepped outside the room momentarily and re-entered with two large metal bowls. He placed them near the table. Water splashed from one of the bowls onto the cement floor as he did. I stared at the other bowl. It almost resembled cereal until the smell struck my nose.

Dog food.

"Eat," the man said. "Drink." He turned his head to the bucket. "Alleviate yourself."

"Please," I said, tears streaming down my face. "Please, let me—"

"This is your home," the man interrupted. "Be a good girl, and I won't... put you down." I screamed. The man raised his shoulders and turned

his face towards the door. "Stop that! Stop that, now!" He grabbed the metal bucket and slammed it against the wall, denting it.
I took a deep breath. I looked at the red eyes of the wolf again. It took me a moment to see two holes below them, where I saw the dark brown eyes of the man staring back at me.

"Don't hurt me," I pleaded, staring at the man's eyes now. “My name is Amber Townsin. My mother is very wealthy,” I lied. “Let me go, and I’ll make sure you're compensated.” The man with the wolf mask shook his head. “She will!” I yelled. “Just… please let me go and—”

"Stop!" the man barked. "That's not your name, anymore. Your name is… ‘girl’ now.” I raised my head and stared at him. “You can be a bad girl or a good girl, that's up to you. Good girls can stay with a master. Bad girls get put down. What will you be?"

I breathed in, my mouth gaping open.

He shook his head again. “You have a lot to learn, girl. Rule one, no screaming. If you do, I’ll put you down like a dog right away. The second, do as I say. The last rule, and this is important… Call me ‘Master’.”

CHAPTER 2

Dawn

"Thank you so much for helping me today. Dawn, was it?" the caller asked.

I smiled, sitting in my cubicle with my headset on. "That's right. I'm glad we were able to resolve your concerns today. Are you happy with our resolution?"

"It's not what I wanted," the man muttered, "but you've been great. What was your last name again? I want to write a good review for you."

"Dawn Nelson, and thank you for your kind words. Have a great rest of your day." I waited for the man to say the same and ended the call, taking off my headset. I took a deep breath, noticing on my computer screen the other twenty-one calls in the queue.

The calls never end. A customer is never truly happy. These were facts of working at a customer service call center that handled complaints. All day I dealt with conflict but did it exceptionally well.

The call that had just ended for example. The man started yelling and swearing almost immediately after I asked him what his name was. Most customer service reps would have hung up, but I managed to turn the call around.

Practically all of the callers were upset because they felt wronged in some way and needed to feel understood. Listening and understanding were the key skills. And when I couldn't manage to empathize with them, I pretended, which was something else I did really well as an actress.

I put on my headset, ready for the next caller, when my friend Sarah Bendry wrapped her arm around my shoulder.

"How do you do that?" she asked.

"What?" I said, adjusting my headset.

"Smiling after a call like that?" She shook her head. "I heard that grumpy old man from across the room complaining about his toaster, and how it broke a week after purchasing it. You tell him it's not covered under warranty, and still somehow manage to smile at the end of the call, and he wants to write you a good review?"

I laughed. "The man shoved a fork into his toaster, fishing out his burnt toast, breaking it. He's lucky he didn't hurt himself, but of course it's not covered. He knew that before he called." I shook my head. "My acting coach told me if you want to pretend to be happy, smiling is the first step. It helps get you in the right state of mind when you need to act the part. Sometimes I even say or think the word 'smile' just to help set the mood. It's the same for all emotions when I act."

Sarah shook her head again. "This job is getting to me. I can't wait to find a new one someday."

Serendipitously, our manager, Ronald walked by as Sarah expressed her dreams of escaping.

"Break, Sarah?" he asked with his usual crappy tone.

Sarah perked up. She plastered a fake smile on her face. "Hey, Ron! Of course I'm on a break. A coffee break... with Dawn." Ronald nodded and continued to walk past us, watching other customer service representatives in their cubicles.

"You're right," Sarah said. "Smiling at Ron makes me not want to choke him with my mouse cord."

"Dark! I like it. What time are you and Vic coming tonight?" I stood up from my desk and tucked in my chair. A coffee break did sound good.

"That's why I popped by," Sarah said with a pout.

"You can't come?" I asked, concerned. It would ruin my surprise party if nobody was there. Sarah and Victor were the only two invited.

"No, of course I'm still coming. Victor was told he has to stay late at work. Only a few hours, though. So we'll be there before eight for sure.

We're excited! Can't believe old man Mike is turning the big four zero."

"Please don't call him 'old man Mike'. Something tells me he'd hate it."

Sarah raised an eyebrow. "Mike? Upset? He's a Zen master. I don't think I've seen that man angry the whole time I've known him."

I could agree to that. Being married to him for over thirteen years, though, I knew when he wasn't himself. The past six months I had noticed changes in his mood, and behaviour. It was almost as if he was never truly present with me. He appeared deep in thought and whatever he was thinking about didn't seem to involve me or our son.

Mid-life crisis, I was told. I never thought Mike would be a victim of one, though.
"He is still the Zen master, or whatever you called him, but lately I think it's bothering him. His age. Everyone he knows is younger than him."

Everyone he knows, I repeated to myself. If only Sarah knew how few people he actually knew. The only friends he really talked to were Vic and Sarah, and that was usually because of my efforts to arrange a double date with them.

His mother had died when Mike was a child, and his father a few years ago.

Besides Vic and Sarah, when he wasn't with me, he was around his brother Rick, much to my dismay. Despite Mike only being a year older, he was lightyears more mature than his little brother.

"Fine," Sarah said. "No 'old man Mike' jokes. 'Papa Mike' jokes, maybe?" I grinned. "Are you doing that smiling acting trick on me now?" she asked, raising her voice with a laugh.

Someone from another cubicle shushed us. I nodded towards the break room. "Coffee?" Sarah nodded back.

The call center room was a large, open space with rows upon rows of cubicles. Each cubicle was partitioned off with cheap, flimsy walls, creating a maze of identical workspaces. The lighting was fluorescent and dim, casting a harsh, unnatural glow over everything. The carpet was old and stained, and the air was stuffy and stale, as if it had never been circulated. It was a miserable place to spend long hours working, and it was no wonder that so many people hated their jobs there.

Along the way I heard others on the phones. I didn't hear my colleagues as much as I did the customers berating them. One woman had her head on her desk, covering herself with her arms. Her body was juddering, and you could hear the faint sound of whimpering.

"This place is getting to me," Sarah said, watching the woman as she walked by. "It gets to everyone, except you."

I rolled my eyes. "She's new right? What's her name?"

"I don't remember," Sarah said. "She won't

last the week at this rate."

I didn't respond. Sometimes it felt like it was everyone for themselves at the call center. With little support from Ron the manager, it was easy to see why. I made a mental note to talk to the new woman later. Hopefully some gentle words of advice could help her stay, if that's what she wanted.

The break room was located just off the main call center floor. It was a cramped and poorly ventilated space, with a few vending machines lining one wall and a small table and chairs in the corner. The table was usually cluttered with half-empty coffee cups, crumpled napkins, and spilled sugar packets. The chairs were uncomfortable and mismatched, and the room had a constant stale smell of old coffee and microwave popcorn. Despite its name, it was not a pleasant place to take a break, and most people avoided it if they could, typically taking theirs at their cubicles.

We entered and made our coffee. I glanced back and saw Ron checking his watch and looking at us.

No wonder why this call center had such a high turnover.

"Vic wanted me to ask if he should bring some cash for poker like last time," Sarah asked.

"I'm sure Mike would love to play," I said. "I'm going to the family cabin early to set up." I smiled again, this time authentically.

"Maybe you can give us a sneak preview of your upcoming play too. What's the date again?" Sarah said. "We still need to purchase tickets."

"I already saved you two. And I'd love to practice my lines. Mike probably knows them better than me at this point. Although he doesn't really set the scene well with his monotone voice." I laughed.

"Lady MacBeth," Sarah said in an old English accent. "It's going to be fun to watch you act Shakespeare."

I nodded in agreement, mouth taut. I had worked hard with the play group to get a lead role. Lady MacBeth was my first. Still though, it wasn't what I really wanted.

"You don't seem so happy about it," Sarah said, raising an eyebrow.

"Lady MacBeth is fun. It's a great part. It's just, I wish women had more interesting roles. I mean, I play a woman overcome with emotions who goes insane. At least I get to play a villain. Bad guys get all the fun lines."

"It would be fun to pretend to be a villain."

"Of course, since I'm a woman villain, everything centers around me being hysterical and acting like a victim." I shuddered. "I hate that. You know, the director of the play told me they're trying to get the rights to make a play from the movie *Misery*. You know, the book by Stephen King."

"Don't know it," Sarah said, which wasn't surprising.

"A woman kidnaps an author, and keeps him until he writes stories the way she wants, with force." I shook my head. "Now that's a villain I would love to play. Just an insanely evil person. That would be fun."

"It sounds more interesting than old man Shakespeare. I never understood why people like him so much. All of his plays end with everyone getting killed."

"A tragedy, it's called in my world. Not all of his plays were."

"The only thing that won't make it a tragedy for me is watching you on the stage."

"Thanks, Sarah."

"I also think Mike and Vic get along so well," Sarah said. "They never hang out much by themselves, though. We need to set up a husband playdate."

I laughed. "Agreed."

"Speaking of play dates, who's watching Mike Junior?"

"My mom and dad," I answered.

"A weekend of fun, games and drinking at a cabin... with no children. This must be heaven for you."

I nodded. "Mike misses Junior when he doesn't spend a lot of time with him during the weekends, though. He's been super busy at work right now."

"Well, people are starting to hand over their

tax info to old man Mike. Accounting season begins." Sarah shrugged. "He's not here. I can't call him that when he's not present?"

"I'm sure Mike, the Zen master, can sense your comments," I said, chuckling.

"I'm sorry we'll be there late. Vic and I can't wait to spend the weekend with you guys, though. Celebrate with young man Mike."

"I can't wait to surprise him with everything," I said.

At that moment, I was so happy. Ready for a weekend of fun with good friends. Our time at the family cabin was going to be a surprise indeed for different reasons. It would be a weekend talked about by news channels and reporters for months to come.

CHAPTER 3

After work, I ran to my car in a frenzy, excited to get to the cabin. Mike said he would drop off Junior at my parents after his workday finished. He still didn't know what I had planned for him or that we were even going to the cabin. I had him promise to be ready for a fun date night.

"You're working too hard," I told him the evening before. "We need a fun night. Just us."

Mike reluctantly agreed. He was more stubborn during tax time. Being an accountant, this was the start of his busy season. It was February, though, and knowing his business I knew the busier nights would be coming. At this time of year, he was still able to enjoy most weekends with me and Junior. The next few months he would spend mostly working, day and night.

I sighed, thinking of it as I drove.

Knowing his work the way I did made me worried. Lately he'd been saying he needed to work some nights at the office. Other times he made excuses to leave the house, usually when Junior was in bed. He said most nights that he was going out with his brother Rick. Sometimes I wondered if that was true, though.

Did he just want to be alone?

How much time would anybody want to spend with Rick, after all? The man was obnoxious. A drunk. I had to use my smile technique every time I saw him to stand the man. It was no wonder he was single at thirty-nine.

"I have no interest in having a woman," Rick had told me on several occasions. I believed it was the other way round. I didn't think many women wanted much to do with Rick.

How could Mike's mother create him and Rick from the same womb? Two totally different people. Mike was successful. He'd become a partner at his accounting firm in his twenties because of the hard work he put in.

Rick made near minimum wage when he was employed, which was seldom. He wasn't the employable type. He had a tendency to tell his bosses to F-word off on occasion. Although sometimes that was something I admired him for. It was a fantasy to tell Ronald what I truly thought of him and his management abilities.

As I drove to the cabin I continued to think about Mike. What was happening to my husband? He moped around the house most of the time. We were less intimate than usual. We weren't arguing more though, which was seldom.

It was almost as if he was waving the white flag. Giving up.

The worst part was I couldn't get him to talk about it. When I asked him what was wrong, he would give short answers. I'm just tired. Hard day at work. Or my favourite answer, "Nothing's wrong."

He would do anything but talk to me about what was happening.

For the first time in my marriage, I was worried about us. Did he still love me? Did he want to stay in this marriage? It was what I wondered daily around him.

The worst part was, I'd thought we were happy. I thought our marriage was... perfect.

Mike only seemed happy when playing with Junior now. No matter how he was really feeling, he was a good father. When he spent time with his son you got the sense they were the only two people in the world. Junior was a young boy and still saw his father as Superman. I was thankful that he didn't see the side of Mike that worried me.

Mid-life crisis, I reminded myself. I'm five years younger than Mike. Perhaps I'll feel the same as I get closer to forty and my thirties are in the rear-view mirror.

Mike was not the type of person who would be open to counseling. His father was a hard man, and counseling made you weak. Only women could have emotions apparently.

It was easy to understand why his brother Rick was the way he was when you met his father.

Truthfully, I never enjoyed the company of Albert Nelson. The nights that Mike did open up to me about his childhood, I could tell his father was a cold man. Mike's mother left his family when he was six years old and never returned. All he had was his father to support him. Mike basically raised Rick himself.

When Albert passed away from a heart attack three years ago, Mike surprisingly took it well. Now, he barely mentioned his father.

My cell phone rang, breaking me from my thoughts. It was the birthday man himself.

"Hey!" I said excitedly.

"Hey," Mike answered. "I'm glad you talked me into having a date night. I really can't wait for it to be just me and you tonight."

I took a deep breath. "Bad day?"

"Did I tell you I hate numbers?"

"That's a real problem if you're an accountant."

Mike laughed. "It certainly is."

I smiled, nearly not turning with the road. Despite saying he only wanted to spend time with me, he seemed playful today. Maybe I had caught him on a better day. Maybe with his actual birthday coming next week, he'd come to grips with whatever was troubling him.

"Hey, Mom!" Mike Junior yelled.

"Hey, Junior!" I yelled into my phone. "Are you excited to go to Grandma's today?"

"Yep! Grandpa said he's taking me to a hockey game tomorrow. The Flames are playing the Goddamn Oilers, he told me."

"Hey!" Mike said to him. "I agree with Grandpa but no bad words, mister."

"Sorry," Junior said in a low voice.

"He's excited," Mike said. "And I'm excited for tonight."

I honked at a car ahead of me when they turned into my lane and nearly struck me. "Sorry! I'll be ready soon too. I just need to set up and we'll be—"

"Set up?" Mike repeated. "Where are you going?"

I sighed audibly. "I can't keep a secret very well. We're going to the family cabin for the weekend!"

"What?" he said, slightly annoyed. "I thought we were going into the city for a date night."

"What's wrong?" I asked. "You love going to the cabin. We haven't been in a few weeks."

"We're supposed to get heavy snow this weekend. Didn't you check the weather?"

"No..." I admitted. "I just want you to have a fun weekend."

"Well, let's just go to the city instead of the cabin," he said. "I wanted to try this new Italian place."

I sighed again. "I'm almost there," I lied.

"At the cabin?" Mike asked.

"Are you really mad at me, or something?" I asked. "I thought you would be happier. I wanted to surprise you."

"You didn't have to surprise me by going to the cabin."

"It's just Sarah and Vic are coming. I wanted us to have a good time together."

"Tell them to come out for dinner," Mike said. "We can hang out at home after. I have to get back at Vic for beating me in poker last time anyway."

I felt my plans crumbling before my eyes. I wanted a fun weekend at our family cabin, and that's what we were going to get. A whole weekend with friends and good times was just what my marriage needed.

"Well Vic and Sarah are already on their way too," I lied. "So please?"

"Stop fighting!" Junior yelled in a playful tone.

"We're not, kiddo," Mike said. This time he made an audible sigh. "Fine. I'll see you soon." Before I could say anything, Mike ended the call.

CHAPTER 4

Thirty minutes after my call, I actually was near the cabin, and exited the highway down a bumpy, wooded dirt road. The tires of my car crunched through the thick layer of ice and slush. The trees on either side were barely visible beneath the blankets of snow that had accumulated on their branches.

It was always the part of the trip to the cabin I hated because of how uneven the road was. Once I made the mistake of attempting to drink a coffee on this trail when Mike and I drove here. Most of the black liquid stained my white sweater instead of making it to my lips. Mike laughed the entire twenty minutes it took to get to the cabin.

As I drove, I looked out into the dense forest. The sun beamed between the trees at me. This area of Kananaskis country wasn't as popular as the more well-known town of Banff, a tourist mecca. It was quieter. The only people who visited these areas were the few who owned property.

When you visited the cabin, it was as if you

were escaping the world. It was just you and nature, and whoever you brought with you. That was all you had to keep you company. Mike and I even had a rule to prevent the outside world from invading our cabin.

No phones. I would usually collect his cell from my reluctant husband, who would attempt a mild defence before giving it to me.

Mike loved it out here. The family cabin used to be his father's. He inherited it after his dad passed away. It took a lot of redecorating, but we had finally made the cabin what we always dreamed: a vacation home that many wished they could have.

We had removed his father's hunting trophies. I gave everything a fresh coat of paint. I chose a warm, earthy color for the walls and a crisp white for the ceiling and trim.

I changed the furniture. I found a beautiful, reclaimed wood coffee table and two matching end tables at a local artisan market, and paired them with a cozy grey sectional and a plush white shag rug.

Finally, I hung up some of my own artwork and added some personal touches, like candles and throw pillows in shades of blue and green.

Outside, the cabin might have seemed the same, but inside was given a personality change. Even Mike was impressed but admitted his father would have hated what I did with the home.

When money was tight over the past few years, I had tried to get Mike to turn the home into a vacation rental. We didn't go every weekend. Usually, it was more like once a month, so why not make some extra dollars from it? I thought my accountant husband would have seen the extra revenue potential, but he was always against it.

It was his family's cabin. He didn't like the idea of strangers staying there.

Sometimes, when work was too much, I thought of coming out here by myself for a while. I never did, though. As much as I loved being in the middle of nowhere, I liked to have company when I did.

Once, I hiked by myself while Mike and Junior slept in. I knew the rule the park rangers told visitors. Make noise when you go on a hike, especially when you're by yourself. Let the animals who live here know that you're coming so you don't surprise them, and they don't surprise you. It was summertime. I rounded a bend in the trail and saw them.

Tiny cubs.

They couldn't have been older than a month or two, I thought. My mouth dropped and I wanted to immediately run over to them, squeeze and cuddle them. I blamed television shows and soft teddy bears for those thoughts. The ones that came immediately after were much scarier.

Where was mama bear?

I quickly made my way back, and thankfully never met her. Mike told me I was lucky. Mama bear was likely there but for whatever reason, didn't see or charge at me.

That day I learned a valuable lesson: respect nature.

I turned down the gravel road that led to our cabin. After another few minutes I had finally arrived. It was a small cabin, only two bedrooms, a living room, kitchen and bathroom. The basement was spacious as well, but mostly used as storage. It was all my family needed, though.

When I parked in front of the cabin, I smiled, thinking of all the trips my family had here the past few years. Mike said someday Junior would inherit the home too. He hoped it would be passed down generations to come.

I stepped out of the vehicle, taking in the smells of the forest. I stood among the tall trees, my nose filled with the crisp, cold scent of the winter woods. The sun was low in the sky, casting a golden glow over the snow-covered landscape. I closed my eyes and took a deep breath, savoring the aroma of pine and frost that filled the air. As I exhaled, a cloud of steam escaped my lips and dissipated into the icy air.

I opened my eyes and gazed around at the surrounding forest, taking in the beauty of the barren branches and the sparkling snow. The only sound was the crunch of my boots on the frozen ground and the occasional rustle of the wind through the trees. I wrapped my scarf more tightly around my neck.

I nearly jumped when I heard a faint noise from the bushes behind the cabin. The sound got louder, until I recognised Taylor Swift. I saw a figure moving on the path. There were so many hiking trails, including the one right beside our cabin.

"Dawn?" the man called out. From his raspy voice I knew immediately it was our not-so-close neighbor, Harold Vaughn.

"Hey, Harold!" I yelled back. I watched as Harold, who was in his late sixties, walked slowly up to me. He had a walking stick in his right hand and a rifle strapped over his left shoulder. I stared at the gun, trying not to show my disdain for it.

Harold was a hunter, even if it wasn't hunting season, so him having a weapon on him shouldn't have upset me, but it did. I smiled, using my acting coach's advice, and Harold smiled back.

As he got closer, I saw he wore a small radio on his back. A smart idea, I thought, given my encounters. Taylor Swift didn't seem the type of music the older man would enjoy, though. His cabin was further down the path. He was widowed, with no children. Unlike the others, his cabin was where he lived year-round.

He enjoyed living off his land. My smile waned as he got closer. I hated the idea of him walking nearby with a weapon. Mike said he had talked to him about hunting near our cabin before when I brought up concerns.

Guns in general made me uncomfortable. I didn't think hunting was morally wrong, it's the presence of the gun itself that bothered me.

"Are you by yourself?" Harold asked, as he left the path and approached me. "Where's Mike?"

"Should be coming soon," I said. "We're celebrating his fortieth birthday today."

Harold nodded. "Young man," he said with his raspy voice and ugly grin. A smile was usually something that lightened someone's facial features. Somehow his made him worse.

I tried my best to maintain eye contact as he spoke. It was difficult, however, as my gaze kept drifting to his mouth. His teeth were yellow and crooked, and I could imagine what his breath would smell like.

"I didn't think I'd have company this weekend," he continued. He glanced at our cabin and back at me.

"We'll be sure to keep it down out here," I said with a laugh.

He looked back at the cabin. "I don't see you guys out here so much lately."

"Right," I said in agreement. "It's tax season now, so Mike's pretty busy. The holidays were busy too. Junior's in second grade now. I wish we had more time to come out here."

"I think Mike may have one of my fishing

rods in the basement," he said, changing the subject abruptly. "Maybe I can grab it." He smiled again.

"Sure. I just need to get ready for his get-together though. Can you come back later?"

"Get-together?"

"Just another couple. Don't worry, I won't have a party out here." I laughed again, this time uncomfortably. This was the longest conversation I had ever had with Harold, and I hoped it was nearly over.

He nodded again, shuffling the gun on his shoulder. "Well, I hope he enjoys his birthday. Please share that with the young man."

"I will, thanks," I said. With a last nod he made his way back to the path behind the cabin and continued his hike. I watched him leave as I took out my luggage from the car and grabbed a plate of baked goods I'd brought.

Harold continued up to the walking trail behind our cabin, not looking back.

CHAPTER 5

I stepped inside the cabin, locking the door behind me. I turned and dropped the bag in front of the couch and put the plate of cookies on the kitchen table. Opening the luggage, I sorted through the clothes I brought for Mike and me until I found the envelope of photographs.

They were all Mike at different ages. I thought it would be fun to have a collage of his life. I picked up the oldest. It was a black and white photo of Mike in diapers. His mother was holding him against her chest, and he seemed content as can be. I made sure to be delicate with it since it was one of the only Mike had with his mom.

I couldn't help but smile as I gazed at the photo. My husband was so small and innocent, with a chubby face and a tuft of dark hair on his head. His mother was looking down at him with a warm, loving expression, and it was clear that she adored him.

I had purchased a frame with metal wires across it. On the wires were miniature clothespins that you could hang pictures on. The first one I put on was Mike with his mother. I smiled again at my husband and his mother. It made me think of my son, Junior.

The day I told Mike I was pregnant was still easy to recall. I had never seen someone so happy in their life as I had when I told Mike we would be having a child. We had tried for over six months to conceive, but it wasn't easy. We were considering talking to a specialist for help. Mike was already blaming himself.

Then it happened, and I told him, and that memory of his happiness would forever be ingrained in me.

I wish I understood why Mike hadn't been himself the past few months. When I thought of that memory of the first time he knew he was going to be a father, I had faith we could get over whatever was happening.

I hung up more pictures in the frame. In one of them Mike was graduating from high school, with a terrible mullet that thankfully he didn't have anymore. Another one was of him in front of his first truck. His brother Rick had his arm wrapped around his shoulder and they grinned for the photo. This time it was Rick sporting the mullet, which again, thankfully he'd moved on from.

The next picture was one of him and his brother standing on either side of his father, who sat on a leather chair. His father's features were hard and demanded respect. Even from the picture I felt how I did when I was a younger woman, visiting him at his home.

His father would not say very much, especially to me. I assumed he hated me. It was on our wedding day I thought differently. Albert had told me he had never seen his son so happy as he did then. He didn't smile when he said it. It was as if he was stating a fact. The sky is blue. The earth is round. And my son is happy.

It was the most endearing thing I had heard his father say.

I continued to hang the photos in the frame. A few of us when we were younger. One of me pushing wedding cake to his nose. Another of Junior, in diapers, held proudly by Mike.

It was at this time he had started to wear his now infamous thick black-framed glasses. Some people said he looked like a more handsome version of Drew Carey.

When the collage was finished, I regarded it with pride. These were snapshots of my husband's life, all of them full of love. I couldn't wait for him to see it.

I threw out the envelope in the garbage under the sink in the kitchen and moved around the cabin. I had gotten into a habit of always checking each room whenever we visited. We had no security system, and it was in the middle of nowhere. I worried someone would break in and steal from us, or I would come to the cabin to find graffiti everywhere.

I walked around the living room and opened the kitchen, content that everything was in order. The small television was where it should be. You couldn't view channels on it. There was no reception in the area. We were only able to use it to watch DVDs. The DVD player was still beside the television. The natural wood floor remained as beautiful as it had last time.

Despite the chilly weather outside, the indoor temperature was comfortable. The triple-paned windows I'd had Mike install helped with that. Still, I fixed the thermostat to make it a little cozier. The brick fireplace against the wall still had burnt logs from our last use.

I went into the guest room, which was his father's bedroom at one time. Although it was bigger than the room we slept in, Mike never felt comfortable sleeping there. It was Junior's room when we came together as a family. Although, Junior would usually wind up in our bed at some point in the night no matter what we tried to bribe him with to stay in his room. For the first time, it would be used for a guestroom for Victor and Sarah.

I went into the main room, bringing in the small case of clothes I brought for Mike and me and stuffing the clothes into the dresser.

I went back to the kitchen and opened the fridge. There wasn't much except condiments. I had enough time to run to the small town of Canmore nearby and grab some more supplies. Steak was Mike's favourite. They had a nice butcher shop where we enjoyed getting our cuts of meat.

I would grab a case of beer for Mike and Vic, and a few bottles of wine for Sarah and me. I smiled, thinking how much fun we would have tonight and over the weekend. I opened a drawer and found a notepad and pen. The first page was filled with a to-do list of things that needed fixing in the cabin.

I turned the page and wrote a message to Mike letting him know I would be in town grabbing food and supplies, and to call me if he got to the cabin before I returned. I ripped out the page and placed it on the kitchen table.

Reaching into my pocket, I grabbed my cell phone, checking the time. I should be able to get back before Mike arrived. I remembered what he said about the weather conditions. I opened up a browser to check. Sure enough, he was right. It was expected to snow heavily all weekend. I didn't see any warnings of blizzard conditions, though. I hoped we'd be okay to leave on Sunday without too many issues.

For a moment I thought about cancelling everything, like Mike had wanted. What would happen if we were all stuck in the cabin for longer than the weekend because we were snowed in, and the roads weren't cleared?

That was when I heard a thud. A loud noise coming from the basement. I froze and listened. I knew the furnace could make sounds sometimes, but this was different.

I was hesitant to investigate it at first. I had read a story of a woman who found a bear hibernating under her cabin porch. I grinned at how silly Mike would think I was if I told him I was scared to go into the basement. At worst, it could be a small animal. A skunk would certainly ruin my weekend plans.

I left my cell on the kitchen table and walked to the stairs. I flicked the light switch and peered down the narrow flight that led to the basement.

CHAPTER 6

Amber

When I heard the footsteps upstairs, I shivered. He was back.

It had been hours since he left me in the basement. It was cold. With my hands chained behind my back it was harder to stay warm. At times I would pace around the small room, as much as the chains would allow. I tried to think of how I could get out. The handcuffs were too tight against my wrists to tug them off.

When I was younger, I watched a horror movie where a woman broke her hand and fingers to slip off handcuffs. I took a deep breath remembering that the woman in the movie was eventually murdered by the killer, despite getting free.

Even if I could get free of the handcuffs and the chain, there was the door issue.

I'd heard him slide a deadbolt on the other side before leaving. How could I get out of the room? The door looked to be made of thick wood.

Breaking down doors in movies seemed so easy, but I knew that wouldn't be the case for me. With no shoes, I would be the one broken if I attempted it.

Footsteps continued upstairs, moving across the main floor above me. I felt a tear coming down my face.

I breathed in deep and tightened my lips.

Don't give him a show. Don't let him see your tears. That's exactly what he wants.

I looked at the dog food. He wants me to drink and eat like a dog. He wants me to do everything he wants.

He wants me to be afraid. The idea of the power he thought he had made me enraged.

I still hadn't eaten a piece of dog food. Even when he yelled at me to do so, I didn't listen. The cold eyes of the wolf's mask stared back at me without a change of expression, but I could tell that under that mask, he was upset.

I wasn't playing the victim too well. He likely wanted me to beg him. Eat the pieces of kibble at his feet and sip my water, thanking him and asking for more. Even though I couldn't see his face, I knew he would smile if I listened like a good little dog that he wanted me to be.

When that realization struck me, and I had come to terms with my situation, I forced myself to stop weeping. That was when he ordered me to eat the dog food. I told him no.

He yelled. I refused, screaming back at him.

He told me to be quiet. I knew that meant there could be someone outside that could hear me. I just had to wait for an opportunity.

When I kept refusing his demands, he walked closer to me, and stopped, standing over me. The man was tall, easily over six feet. I waited for him to do something.

I knew what happened to young women who were kidnapped. I'd heard true crime stories of what monstrous things men would do to women.

Instead, the man just looked at me. He waited for me to stare up at him. When I did, I saw the mask slots and his real eyes staring back at me.

"You better start doing what I say, little doggy," he said in a deep voice. "Or the pain will start." He left immediately after, locking the door behind him.

Now he was back. The pain, he said, would soon start. The footsteps continued upstairs. Soon he would come and visit me, I knew.

He's come back to... put me down. He wants me to be afraid. He wants me to be scared for my life.

Maybe fighting back was better than playing along with whatever sick game he has for me.

I stood up from my chair and kicked it hard. It slammed on the floor. I kicked it again, sliding it across the cement.

I was about to shout all the curse words I could when I heard footsteps coming down the stairs. The pace was slow. It was as if he knew the build up of terror I had brewing in me was too much to handle. I hated him so much for that.

An image of my mother struck my mind.

I should have answered my phone when she called the night I was taken, but I didn't. I was too stubborn to pick it up. I wanted her to learn her lesson.

And what stupid reason did I have for not wanting to talk to my mother? We'd got into an argument over politics. Her worldview was so different to mine. I hated it, especially now when education had really opened my eyes to the world I lived in.

I should have answered the phone. I would have told her how much I loved her. I would have apologised for how stupid I was for ignoring her. Who cared about her worldviews that had nothing to do with my personal life?

I was stupid for making that a reason not to talk to her. For not telling her how much I loved her. For raising me as a single mother after she divorced my father.

Then I thought of him, my dad.

If he had called me before I was taken, I would have readily picked up the phone, to curse at him.

He was an abusive man who'd hurt my mother continuously. My mom would hide me in my room when she knew he was in a mood. I used to think it was because she didn't want me to see my dad that way. When I was older, I knew the truth: she didn't want me to get hurt as well.

When I was twelve, I gave my number to Cody Bobbery, the most handsome boy in class. I never thought he would call. He was the popular kid in class, and I wasn't. But he did call, only my father picked up the phone.

That evening he struck me in the face and called me a whore.

The next day, mom packed two bags and we left while he was at work.

I had never seen or spoken him again since that night. I tried to talk my mom into calling the police, but she told me not to provoke my father. I was so angry at my mom for letting him get away with what he had done to us.

My father, the monster, was gone from my life for good after that. Once in a while, my mother would tell me something about him. I would tell her I didn't care to know anything.

Apparently, my father moved on from us too. Mom found out he remarried and had another child. I pitied the kid. They would find out the hard way what their father was, a monster.

I hadn't thought of my dad in some time...

That was until now, in the basement, as the monster was coming back to me.

My tears could not be resisted any longer and streamed freely down my face. All I wanted was to see my mother. I thought of the fear I had when my father struck me that night because little Cody Bobbery called me at home.

In between sobs, I sat on the cement floor, turning my head away from the door, and closed my eyes. I didn't want to see him again. Not with that mask on.

"Please!" I shouted. "Master... don't hurt me!"

I heard the deadbolt slide back, and the door slowly opened.

CHAPTER 7

Dawn

I took my first few steps into the basement. I hated the narrow stairs, and the tight walls on either side. I felt like I was spelunking. On one visit, when Junior was a few years younger and much more uncoordinated, he managed to fall down the entire flight. He cried on the cement floor at the bottom uncontrollably. I ran to my son, but Mike was even faster, managing to sprint down the steps and check on him.

Junior's ring finger was bent in an unusual way, and we had to bring him immediately to the nearby hospital in Banff. There wasn't much the emergency room doctor could do but set the finger properly and cast it.

I was so upset at myself for not seeing the potential for Junior to hurt himself. Mike was different. These things happen, he told me. When we came back to the cabin, Mike grabbed a permanent marker and wrote Junior's name on the finger cast, which made him smile.

When I got to the bottom of the stairs, I shivered from the cold cement floor. I pulled on a string from the ceiling, turning on the light. The room was full of junk and outdoor gear.

It was likely stuff we should have brought to the town dump, but instead decided to shove it in the cabin basement. A few of the boxes were Mike's father's. Mike was too sentimental to throw those out, and I couldn't blame him.

A two-person kayak leaned against the wall with the paddles underneath it. Snowshoes hung from a hook. Beside them were several fishing poles. I studied them, thinking of Harold. I saw Mike's that he always used. Beside his was Rick's pole, which I used sometimes. The small one belonged to Junior. I looked around the room to see if there was another.

That's when I noticed the butcher room door was closed. It was my least favourite room in the cabin. It was where Mike's father and his sons would process the carcass of whatever they'd hunted. They even had a metal table to lay the dead animal on.

I never went to the cabin with Mike when his father was alive. It was only after, when we inherited it, that we would go as a family. The butcher door was typically open.

Not only was it closed, but it was locked from the outside with a deadbolt. I shook my head, wondering why they would want to install a deadbolt on the outside of the door. Were Mike and his family afraid the dead animals would stand up and escape?

Thankfully, Mike hadn't been hunting in years. Even before his father passed, Mike didn't go. I remembered when his brother Rick would ask him, and Mike would decline politely. Rick would always call him a pussy. I cringed, thinking of their exchanges. Mike was very mature, and Rick... was anything but. It was hard for me to understand their relationship at times.

"Please!"

I stared at the wooden door as if it had spoken to me. I shook my head in disbelief. It sounded like a woman.

"Master, don't hurt me!"

I froze in place, staring at it. I heard someone crying from the other side. I patted my jeans pocket and realized I left my cell phone upstairs. The sound of sobbing rose in volume.

"I can't!" the person cried out. "I can't do this! I need my... mother!"

When she said those words, I sprung to the door, sliding back the deadbolt. I pushed the door gently. My eyes widened when I saw her.

A young woman, wearing a stained white sweater, sat on the floor. Her head was turned away from me.

"I can't do this," the woman said between tears. She couldn't have been much older than twenty I guessed from her appearance. I noticed the University of Calgary sweater. That's when I saw the chain behind her. Her arms were behind her back, as she rocked back and forth on the floor.

I opened my mouth to say something, but no words would escape.

The girl turned her head and stared at me with fear. "Who are you?" she asked, her eyes wide. She stood up quickly, and I took a few steps back. "No – don't leave," she cried. "Please, call the police."

"Who are you?" I asked, my eyes wider than before. I looked at the floor and saw what appeared to be dog food scattered across it.

Before she could answer, I heard the front door upstairs open and close with a thud.

"Dawn!" It was unmistakably Mike hollering. "I'm here!" Where are you?"

I met the young woman's eyes, which were just as wide as mine. I took a deep breath. "Please," she whispered, "don't let him hurt me."

I glanced back at the stairs in shock. "Stay quiet," I whispered, closing the door quietly and sliding the deadbolt across.

CHAPTER 8

I quickly made my way to the staircase, staring up it. There was too much to process and no time for me to take it in. All I could think about was one question.

Who was she?

"Dawn!" Mike called out from upstairs. "Where are you?"

I put my foot on the first step.

Who was she?

Why was she locked up in the basement of our cabin?

I heard Mike walk around, the floors creaking with each step. He was getting closer to the stairs.

Smile, an inner voice demanded of me. Smile.

I listened to my gut, putting on a smile, and hurried up the stairs.

"Hey, Mike," I said when I got to the top. He was in the living room and turned to me, fixing his thick glasses.

"There you are," he said. I studied his face

intently and searched for any clue that he knew I found her. When he saw my wide, greeting grin he returned it with his own. I had been married to Mike for thirteen years and saw his smile most days.

That day it was as if the man smiling back at me was a stranger.

Who was she? What did Mike do to her?

"You got here quickly," I said. "I wasn't expecting you for another hour or so. Now you ruined the set-up as well as your surprise."

Mike chuckled. "I do like ruining things, sorry."

He stood across the room from me. We faced each other, several meters apart. I suddenly realized I wasn't playing the part of the wife of a birthday man very well. I walked up to my husband and wrapped my arms around his waist, giving him a tight squeeze. I looked up at him and gave him a quick kiss.

I am of short stature. Mike on the other hand was over six feet. Sometimes he complained of back pain when he lowered himself to kiss me. Today he smiled. I smiled back, but inside I felt nauseous.

"Happy birthday," I said lovingly. "Well, birthday party I suppose."

"I'm happy that I changed my mind," Mike said. He looked down at the kitchen table, at the collage I had made. He picked it up slowly, taking his time to relive every memory. "This is...

beautiful, really," he said. "I can't believe the wife I have sometimes."

I can't believe my husband either, I thought to myself. "I've been working on that since I got here."

Mike lowered the frame. He continued to gaze at the pictures when he asked, "Why were you in the basement?" He glanced up at me when I took my time answering.

"Our cabin neighbor, Harold Vaughn," I managed. "He was hiking when I got here. He mentioned he thought his fishing rod was in the basement."

Mike laughed. "No, it's not."

"Well, he wanted me to tell you happy birthday, anyway."

"That was nice of him."

"How was Junior when you dropped him off at my mother's?" I asked, thinking of anything to say besides screaming in terror about the woman trapped in my basement, and my husband who put her there.

Mike smiled when I mentioned our son's name. "Excited. All they do is sit around all night and watch television with him, but he loves it."

Mike put down the frame and appeared to wipe a tear from his eye. "Dawn," he said in a low voice. He looked at me in a way I had never seen before. I couldn't tell if he would grin next or explode with rage.

"Is... everything okay, Mike?" I asked. "You seem out of it." The statement made my insides roll. *I* was out of it.

"I..." Mike struggled with his words. It was strange to see. "I'm sorry."

My smile vanished now. There was no need to act. The look on his face would have troubled me despite what I found in the basement.

"What are you saying, Mike?" I said, taking a step back. "You're scaring me."

Mike shook his head. "I'm sorry, I haven't been myself."

"Who have you been?"

"A sad man. Life... is so fleeting. Junior is growing up so fast, but so am I." A tear rolled down his face. I stared at him, trying to understand, until I realized I needed to comfort him. I grabbed his arm and snuggled into his chest.

"I know you've been wanting your space lately," I said. "What can I do to help you?"

Mike studied the collage. "You can tell me the truth."

I let go of his arm and looked up at him. "What truth?"

"All these memories I have when looking at this collage. In every picture I'm smiling, but I'm not sure if I was really happy in many of them." He put a finger on the picture of his mother and him. "I don't think I was until I met you. Until we had Junior. But now... I feel different. Forty," he said, shaking his head. “I remember when I was a teenager making fun of men in their forties who were paper-pushers, doing nothing with their lives, and now I am one.” He turned to me, not trying to hide his emotion for a change. “I’m worried. My father didn’t make it to his seventies. My grandpa died in his fifties from a heart attack. My life is already half over. I’ve been thinking about life a lot lately. I worry that I haven't used mine to the fullest.”

“No, Mike,” I said. I grabbed the collage from his hand and placed it on the table. “You are a good man.” I had said it from impulse, not thinking of the girl downstairs. Up until today I had never questioned the kind of man he was. “You’re a good father,” I said. That was an easy statement to make. “And a good husband. This life is all about the memories we make with the people that we love.” I pointed at the collage. “These are only a few with your people who love you.”

Mike lowered his head and wiped a tear. He laughed. “Ah, so emotional today. It's everything you’ve done for me. I wasn’t expecting your present. It really got to me. Seeing my mother and father. Rick. Us. Junior. I really have an amazing wife. And you set up a little get-together for me.” He looked outside at the snow that continued to fall. “Speaking of Vic and Sarah, are we sure they’re coming? The snow is starting.”

“She said she would no matter what but will

be a little late because of Vic's work."

Mike nodded. I spotted my cellphone on the edge of the table, and quickly grabbed it. Mike opened the fridge.

"No beer," he said.

"I was about to make a trip into town," I said, my voice cracking, slipping my phone into my jeans pocket and heading towards the bedroom. I opened the door and quickly closed it behind me. I felt my hand shaking uncontrollably.

I took a deep breath and took out my phone. 911. What would I even say?

Before I could dial, Mike opened the bedroom door and looked at me. It was the same face he'd worn in the kitchen. I wasn't sure if I should scream or smile.

"Phones!" he said in a funny tone. "You know the rules, no phone." He grabbed my cell quickly from my hands and gave me a playful grin. "Cabin rules."

CHAPTER 9

Mike poured a glass of scotch and put the bottle under the kitchen sink where he hid it. He grabbed a cigar from his winter jacket pocket and opened the front door to light it. It was his tradition. It was something he, his father and brother would do at the start of a trip to the cabin.

I walked around the cabin, tidying up, pretending to get ready for our guests, while trying to sort out in my mind what to do.

He puffed on the thick stack of tobacco while staring off into the forest. Eventually he sat outside on the porch and closed the door behind him.

I always hated the Nelson family tradition. The stink of a cigar was unbearable to my virgin lungs. Traditionally, though, the Nelson family would smoke inside the home. Once Mike and I inherited the cabin we made a rule of no smoking inside. Mike was more worried about second hand smoke when it came to Junior.

His time outside gave me an opportunity to think. The young woman in the basement. I had automatically assumed Mike was the one who put her there.

What if it wasn't him, though?

We kept a fake rock with a housekey inside, completely obvious to anyone, outside in the landscaped front of the cabin. Someone could have found it and used the home for whatever he planned to do with the woman in the basement.

Not very many people found their way around these woods except those who owned a cabin.

That made me think of Harold. He was hiking by the house when I arrived. How often had I seen him when we went to the cabin? Only a few encounters at best. He lived by himself, though. If he were to have kidnapped a woman, why wouldn't he keep her in his own home?

None of it made sense.

All I could think about was the girl. What terrible things had someone done to her? Was that someone my husband?

I watched Mike from inside the cabin, puffing out a thick cloud of smoke.

He seemed like he didn't have a care in the world. Besides his emotional exchange when he got here, he seemed happy as ever. Almost like his old self.

I thought of the young woman again. She was scared, rightfully so. She was dirty, but she didn't seem hurt in any way I had noticed. Physically at least.

I needed to know who she was, why she was there, and if my husband put her there.

Mike puffed out a white wall of smoke from his cigar. I breathed in deep, seeing how he was. If he had kidnapped the girl, why was he acting like nothing had happened?

Perhaps Mike was the better actor in our marriage than me.

Just talk to him, I thought. This can't be Mike. He is not a violent man. He never fought anyone, besides his brother growing up. He never raises a hand to Junior or me. He was emotional when he told me about the abuse his father would dish out to him when he was a child.

Then again, he hasn't been himself lately. Working late, leaving the house by himself for hours at a time. How do I know he was even at work today? He works remotely at times.

"Don't let him hurt me."

Those were the last words the girl said to me before I locked her back in the room.

The image of her struck me hard this time. The smell of dog food scattered on the floor. The bucket, which could only be used for one thing.

Mike didn't know about my surprise cabin trip. He arrived pretty quickly after I told him about it. He should have taken at least another hour.

As soon as he arrived at the cabin, he took my phone.

The cell phone rule wasn't new. It was in fact

me who'd enforced it the last time we were at the cabin. I snatched his cell when he was checking his stock portfolio. He could have been waiting to do the same with me when I had my phone, waiting to exact his husband's revenge.

I shook my head. Two years ago, we decided to disconnect the cabin's landline. The only way we could communicate with anyone was through our cell phones. It was my idea to save a little money.

As Mike enjoyed his cigar, I attempted to find my phone. There was a good chance he still had it in his pocket, even though that would be against the no phone rule. I searched through the kitchen, opening drawers and checking the usual places we would tuck things.

If I was quick enough. I could run to the washroom, lock the door and call 911, then put the phone back before he finished. It would be a long wait before the police would show, but thankfully he enjoyed thick and long cigars.

"What are we having for supper?" Mike called from outside.

"Uh, I was thinking steak, with Vic and Sarah!" I yelled, closing a cupboard. I hunted around the living room, in between couch cushions.

"Fantastic!" Mike said. "I should have brought another cigar for after dinner."

"That's too bad!" I replied, peering behind the television and DVD player. I couldn't find my phone anywhere.

As if on cue, a cell phone rang. It was a ringtone I knew. 'I've Got You Under My Skin,' by Frank Sinatra. It was Mike's phone. His musical taste was always a few generations behind anything modern. I traced the sound until I discovered it was in the one place I couldn't reach, on top of the fridge.

Mike stood up quickly and stepped inside the cabin. With the cigar still entrenched in his mouth he reached for his phone, looked at the number and smiled.

"Hello, Darlene," he said to my mother. "Thank you, thank you," he said after a moment. "Yes, the big forty this year." He turned to me with a grin. "Yes, your daughter tried to surprise me, although she kind of let the cat out of the bag at the last minute." He nodded and listened. "Junior wanted to call me. Yes, put the kiddo on." He waited for his son to greet him. "Hey Slugger!" he said. "Are you having fun at Grandma and Grandpa's house? Good. What are you doing? Ah – watching television." Mike winked at me. "Thank you, son, for saying happy birthday to me, even though it's next week. You will have to tell me again." His smile grew. "I love you too, kiddo. Okay, Junior, have fun. Do you want to talk to Mom?" He said he loved him again before handing me the phone.

As I watched my husband speak to our son, my heart melted. How could I have ever thought he was capable of doing anything to the woman downstairs? He was my best friend. My partner for life. Here I was, pretending he was some sort of monster.

Mike handed me the phone. I put it to my ear slowly. "Hey, Junior," I said.

"Hey, Mom," he said with a boyish voice. Every year his tone changed more and more as he grew. "We really surprised Dad, didn't we?"

"We sure did."

"Is he happy?"

"He is." I breathed in deep and smiled at Mike as I replied.

"Good, because I know Dad's been... sad. He needs to be happy for his birthday party." I laughed. My boy was so sensitive to the emotions in our home. I tried to not talk about whatever Mike was going through with him. I hoped he hadn't noticed how different his father was acting. I was naive to think he didn't pick up on the emotional tension in the house.

"Mom?" Junior said as a question.

"Yeah, Junior?"

"When it's actually Dad's birthday can we celebrate again? I want to be there for his birthday too."

"Of course. We'll have another party when it's your dad's birthday. Just the three of us." When I said that, Mike's face brightened.

This made me feel even more guilty for the

thoughts I'd had. This was the man I loved. How could I not have faith in him?

"Mommy and Daddy have to go now," I said to Junior shyly. "Goodnight, son. I love you."

"Love you too, Mommy," Junior said.

I ended the call, lowering the phone slowly. I placed it on the table beside the collage.

Mike suddenly realized he still had the cigar in his mouth when he puffed out some smoke, and apologized, heading towards the front door.

"Wait," I said to him. He stopped and smiled at me. "We need to talk." When I showed the concern on my face his expression changed.

"What's wrong?" he asked.

"We need to call—" A loud knock on the door startled me. Mike calmly went to the front door and opened it, smiling wide when he saw who was there.

His brother Rick grinned back at him as Mike opened it wider.

CHAPTER 10

Amber

I sat on the ground, numb to the cold of the cement floor as I listened to the feet stomp above me.

Who was the woman who came downstairs?

Whoever she was, she seemed just as frightened as I did when she found me. The look of disgust she had when she saw the dog food matched how I must have seemed when I saw it at first.

Who was the second person that yelled for her?

Dawn. That was her name.

I tried to think of everyone I could. I didn't know anyone named Dawn. I certainly didn't know the woman herself. Could she be an older friend of a friend? An aunt of someone I knew. A friend of my mom's?

Since I'd awoken in the basement, I'd struggled to keep my emotions steady, switching between crying and being angry.

The man that called for Dawn's voice I didn't recognize. Although the man who wore the wolf head's voice was muffled, it sounded deeper.

Every time they walked around upstairs, I worried that they would be coming back for me. I knew for certain that at some point the man in the mask would return.

The woman might not be someone I knew, and seemed afraid, but who was to say she wasn't involved with the person who kidnapped me in some way. Would she truly help me?

All I knew was that the fear in Dawn's eyes matched my own. She was just as surprised to see me as I was to see her. Hopefully that meant she could help me. Hopefully that meant she would do something.

There was something about the face Dawn made before she left that comforted me. Even the words Dawn said before she left made me feel better.

"Stay quiet," she warned.

These were words I had heard before. Those nights as a child when my father was more upset than usual, and my mother would lock my bedroom door, she would say something similar. My mother even had the same expression of concern Dawn had before closing the door.

That was when it hit me: Dawn wanted to protect me from whoever else was with her.

Those nights my father was enraged, I

would hear him take out his anger on my mother. The thought of it still struck a nerve even over a decade later. At a young age I knew my father was a monster.

Sometimes I struggled to remember what he looked like. It had been so long since I had seen him. I refused to say his name. It was better to think of him as a skeleton in my closet that would never see the light of day again.

My parents weren't married. Me being on this earth happened by mistake. Even though they didn't know each other well, they tried to raise me together. It took my mom years of abuse to realize that was a bad idea.

Sometimes I used to think my mother was weak for staying with my father as long as she did. Sometimes I was angry at her for what I saw growing up and what happened to me.

I hadn't realized the strength it took to leave a man like my father.

I sat in the small room on the cement floor, wishing I could say many things to her. Positive things for a change.

With that thought, I shifted my hands behind my back. I had been moving my chains as I sat, attempting to squeeze my wrists through the cuffs. At one point I thought they'd wiggled, but I was sure it was my mind playing a devious trick, giving me faith that I could escape.

I couldn't remember how long it had been

since I ate or drank. Suddenly the kibble scattered around me seemed more and more tempting.

I looked at the water bowl, leaned forward, and drank. With my hands tied behind me, it was difficult and strenuous. I slid my legs apart to reach the bowl and sipped. I nearly fell, and would have slammed my forehead onto the cement, but caught my balance. I nearly finished the bowl, trying not to think about how stupid I looked.

That was when I thought about it. My chains. The handcuffs.

Could the water act as a lubricant to help slide the cuffs off?

I turned my body to the bowl, and then I heard something new. A third pair of footsteps upstairs.

How many people would be coming to this house? If I called for help, would one of them do something for me? At the very least, Dawn was on my side. Was whoever else at this home a good person?

I thought about calling out, but stopped: what if they were all bad? What would the three of them do to me? What were their plans?

I shook my head and tried not to think about it. I had my own plans. I focused instead on trying to dip my wrists into what remained of the water in the bowl.

CHAPTER 11

Dawn

"Happy birthday, brother," Rick shouted, walking inside and holding Mike tight. "Congrats, old man."

"Please, stop," Mike said with a smile. He took the cigar from his mouth and tossed it outside before the door closed.

"The big four zero, brother. That's a big deal." Rick let go.

"What are you doing here?" I asked.

"Mike mentioned you were coming to the cabin this weekend. I'm hunting with some friends not too far away from here."

"Friends?" Mike repeated and laughed. "Those old men from that online group? The preppers?"

"Preppers?" I asked.

"People who prepare for the end of the world," Rick said. "I don't believe it. I just like to hunt, and have no one else to go with." He sneered at Mike.

Rick walked over to me and gave me a huge bear hug. “Sister!” It was something he had called me since we were married. Rick could be something else at times, but he had an endearing side. He wrapped his arms around me and lifted me off the floor.

I slapped his shoulder, demanding to be put down.

“You guys settled in for the weekend?” he asked.

“We were until you got here,” Mike said. “Now we’d like to leave.”

Rick gave him a sideways look. “Sure, bro.”

Mike raised a hand. “Speaking of old men, Dawn ran into Harold Vaughn today.”

“Man,” Rick said, rubbing his unkempt neck beard, “haven’t seen him since Dad passed. Surprised he’s still alive. Always thought he was a weird dude, to be honest. Not sure why Dad liked him so much.”

“Well, he probably has a better head on his shoulders than those preppers. He’s all by himself now too. You should hunt with him sometime. The old man could use company.”

Rick nodded. “Yeah, it would be nice not to hear about secret governments and coup attempts. He lives in his cabin now, right?”

“I believe so,” Mike said.

“That guy was a beast of a hunter. Remember when he shot that elk from over a hundred and sixty yards? Boom!" he shouted. "Straight in the eye. Big fucker went right down. We were just kids back then. Vaughn had a killer shot. He shot better than Dad did. He definitely loves hunting."

"I had to talk to him a few visits back. He was hunting rabbits near the house. First time I ever got mad at him. He understood when I mentioned Junior, though."

"Dad and he were close."

Mike lowered his head. "They were, yeah."

"How's work?" I asked.

Rick widened his eyes. He always appeared tired. I'd read that shift work was detrimental to someone's health. Despite only working his new job for a few months, Rick always seemed beat, like he could drop at any moment and take a nap. At least he still had a job. He had been working with this employer for nearly a year, which could be a record.

"It's work," Rick answered. He peered at the table. "Cookies!" He immediately brushed past me and grabbed a few.

"The ones with the green dye have nuts in them," I said quickly.

Rick raised an eyebrow. "Good catch, sister." He put a few back on the plate, then went to the kitchen and washed his hands.

He picked up the collage. "Look at us. Good looking people I must say."

"Why did I ever think a mullet was a cool

hairstyle," Mike said, fixing his glasses.

"Probably because you looked so badass with one. Hell, maybe I should bring it back. It suited me." Rick eyed the first picture and lowered the collage. "I didn't know you had a picture of Mom." He paused, studying it again. "Hell, I don't even have a picture of her. Where'd you find it?"

"Found it in Dad's room when we took possession of the cabin," Mike said in a low voice.

Mike hated bringing up ownership of the cabin. It was something he and Rick had fought about. Near the end of Albert Nelson's life, Rick had spent much more time at the cabin than Mike and felt his dad would have wanted the home to go to him, despite what his will read.

It took months for the brothers to get over the issue and talk again.

Mike pursed his lips. "I can make you a copy."

Rick dropped the collage on the table hard. "Why the hell would I want a photo of you and Mom? I don't suppose you found one of me and her?"

Mike shook his head.

Rick nodded. "That's just like Dad, to take a picture of you and Mom, but not me." His jovial demeanor was quickly changing. I had seen Rick upset many times, and it always started with comments like this. "There's another reason I came tonight." He looked at me with a smirk, then at Mike. "I got you a present, brother." Suddenly, he had a happy temperament again.

Mike shook his head. "Oh, boy. A girly magazine again?" he said with a playful tone.

"You were nineteen when I did that. And you weren't getting any." Rick turned to me. "Sorry. He wasn't, though."

"I'm sure women are lining up for you, Rick," Mike said. "When was your last girlfriend?"

Rick laughed. "I get what I need and leave them. Only you have the decency to keep one around after." Rick turned to me again. "Sorry." I shook my head in response. Rick pointed at Mike. "Stop being mean, old man, or I'll have to keep your present for myself."

Rick went back to the table and grabbed a safe cookie for him to eat. He took a large bite, nearly devouring it all, leaving crumbs in his beard. He made an orgasmic sound. "Amazing, sister. Amazing."

"Thanks," I said. I was already getting to my threshold of how much Rick I could handle for the night.

"Do you want to stay?" Mike asked. "We have other friends coming."

"Friends?" Rick repeated.

"Victor and Sarah," I said. "Sarah works with me."

"Sounds too civilized for me, bro." Rick grabbed another cookie. "I just want to give you my gift, sing happy birthday to you, and be on my way. It's in the trunk of my car, your gift," he said, waving his hand. "C'mon, I'll show you."

Mike put on his hiking boots and went outside with Rick.

When they were out of sight, I immediately saw an opportunity.

The girl. I needed to know more.

I quickly but quietly went down the stairs, sliding the deadbolt to the butcher room open. The girl sat on the cement floor, where she was before. She gazed up at me slowly.

"What's your name?" I asked. "Quickly, we don't have much time."

"Amber, Amber Townsin," she replied.

"Who did this to you?" I asked. "How long have you been here?"

"Since last night," she answered. "I don't know who did it. He wore a mask. A head of a wolf."

"A wolf's head?" I was stunned. "My name is Dawn Nelson. My husband, Mike. You heard his voice when he called for me before. This is our cabin. Was it him who took you? Who hurt you?"

Amber took a deep breath. "I don't know. His voice didn't seem as… deep." She stood up, her legs shaking as she did. Her sleeves were soaked. "Did you call the police?"

"I'm trying," I said. "I don't know who to trust." I glanced up at the ceiling. "I can't stay." I ran out of the room and began closing the door. I glanced back at the girl, who seemed defeated.

“Stay quiet. I’ll figure something out.” I closed the door, and the deadbolt, making my way quickly up the stairs.

I was nearly out of breath, but made it just in time, as Mike walked into the cabin holding a black rifle.

CHAPTER 12

Mike raised the gun and aimed around the cabin, looking through the scope with a smile. But as soon as he saw the fear on my face, his expression darkened. My mouth still gaped open.

"What is it?" he asked. "You can't hide your emotions that well, you know. I haven't owned a gun since before I married you."

"Well…" I tried to find the words. He seemed so comfortable with the weapon in his hand. He was so happy to hold it. When he saw my fear, it was as if a light switch had been flicked, and he seemed enraged.

"Rick did something nice," Mike said. "This gun is special." He raised the gun and aimed it towards a wall. "Scope still looks good. I wonder how well it shoots."

Rick came into the cabin, grinned at me, and hugged his brother again. "I can see you already love the gift. Happy birthday again, brother. He wanted you to have it. It was never supposed to be mine."

I watched as Mike turned away and wiped

his eyes.

"Man up." Rick laughed. "Dad would have hated to see you cry holding his favourite gun like that."

Mike joined in. "Yeah, he would have immediately taken it away."

"And called you a pussy, at a minimum." Rick turned to me and shook his head with a smile. "I can see I've upset the missus, so my work here is done." He walked up to me for a hug, and I flinched, taking a step back.

"What's wrong?" Rick said. "Do you hate me that much for getting him a rifle? It's for sentimental value. I doubt Mike would even use it."

I took a deep breath. I thought of the girl in the basement. Now was not a time to make a scene, I knew, no matter how frightened I felt.

A moment ago, I'd been willing to tell Mike about her, but now watching him hold the rifle, I felt... uneasy. I had such a strong feeling that something was wrong.

"You're right, Rick," I said. "Sorry. It's a nice gift." I stepped forward and hugged him one last time. "Enjoy your hunt."

"Always do," he said. He turned to Mike. "Those preppers like to hunt in luxury. We rented a cabin and everything. Our dad was too tough for that. He would make us camp outside."

Mike smiled. "The old man was something else."

Rick nodded. “Well, I ruined your night sufficiently for now.” He turned to me. “Until next time.”

“Thanks, Rick,” Mike said. “Enjoy your weekend.”

“You guys too. If you get bored of your high society friends, let me know. I can always come by.”

Smile, my inner voice told me. I finally managed a wide one. “Good to see you,” I said. “Take a few more cookies for the road.”

Rick’s eyes widened. “Of course, of course. Thanks.” He grabbed a few from the tray, waved and left the cabin. I watched him through the window as he got into his yellow Jeep.

The sound of a click made me turn my head immediately. Mike aimed around the room and pulled on the trigger a few times.

“I can sense you staring at me,” he said.

“I just… Don’t want to keep it in our house. Junior is still too young.”

Mike lowered the gun, and reluctantly nodded. “Fine. I’ll rent a locker somewhere.”

“I don’t even like it in the cabin to be honest.”

Mike rolled his eyes. “Fine, I’ll put it downstairs.”

“No!" I said a little too loudly. Mike turned to me, raising an eyebrow. I thought of a lie quickly. “My gift is down there. I didn’t hide it. I didn’t have time to wrap it before you came.”

“Another gift?” He glanced at the table. “I

thought the collage was my gift." He stared at me intently, watching my reaction, until he smiled. "You are full of surprises. Another gift. What a wife I have." He walked over to the table, moved the collage to the side and placed the gun beside it. "For Junior, I have no problem renting a locker." He studied the pictures. "Boy, if you knew the trouble we got into when we were kids, playing with Dad's guns... You're right. We will keep it in a locker. Thankfully, Junior isn't Rick."

"Something we can both be happy about."

Mike eyed one of the photos. "You know, when Dad died and gave this rifle to Rick, I was heartbroken about it. It's just a gun, I know. It meant a lot to him, though. It was almost his third son. He talked to it. Even gave it a name. *Justice*."

"Justice. Why name a gun Justice?"

Mike laughed. "He never told us. He bought the rifle after the Vietnam War, before coming back to America. His story was he took it from a soldier who tried to kill him, after— Well, you know... It was special to him. It was the only gun he used when he went hunting. I don't think Rick uses it. He likes the more modern rifles. More ammo capacity. Laser attachments. When I did hunt, I liked simple weapons like this." He looked at me. "What did you have to tell me?"

"What?" I was confused.

"Before Rick came, you wanted to tell me something. You seemed concerned." Mike glanced down at the table and picked up a yellow note I'd written for him.

"That's what I wanted to tell you. Vic and Sarah are coming soon. We need supplies. Beer. I wanted to get steak for us." I also needed an opportunity to be alone to call for help. Amber Townsin depended on me.

"Sounds amazing to me. Let's go."

"No," I said. "Stay, enjoy your brother's gift, which you seem to love more than mine."

"Not fair," he said. He grabbed his father's gun. "I wonder if I still have my kit to clean it. I think it's in the basement somewhere with my dads' boxes."

I watched him and thought of Amber. "Maybe it's better you just come with me," I said reluctantly. "You're so picky with your beer and cut of steak we choose."

Mike shook his head. "You never pick a good cut. You don't pay close enough attention when making decisions. You just grab whatever is closest to you. You need to look at the marbleization of the steak. It's thickness."

"Thanks for the lesson," I said, grabbing his jacket from the hook. "Now, let's go." I handed it to Mike.

Finally, he reached for his parka. It was a faded green color, but it had kept him warm through many winters at our cabin. He slipped it on, taking a moment to adjust the hood before turning to me with a grin.

I didn't know what to think. Was Mike responsible for Amber Townsin? If not him, who else?

"Ready," he said, waiting for me. I nodded and put on my boots and jacket.

No matter what was happening, once in town, all 1 needed was enough time to call the police.

Mike turned to me with an expression of concern. "Before we leave, there's something I need to do."

CHAPTER 13

Mike walked ahead of me towards a tall grouping of trees behind the cabin. It was a walk we had done many times. This short hike was the second tradition Mike Nelson had when we visited the vacation home.

As always, he didn't talk much. His head was lowered, and he turned his face from me so I couldn't see his wet eyes.

Finally, we arrived at a large fallen tree. During the summertime it would be covered with moss and other signs of life, but today the snow coated most of it.

Mike walked up to the middle of the fallen tree and looked at me. He reached out his hand. At first, I was reluctant, but knew better than to stop pretending now. Mike was always emotional when we came to his spot.

Seeing him so vulnerable was something I used to find touching. After discovering Amber in the basement, I wasn't sure what to think anymore.

I walked up beside him and wrapped my arm around his waist.

"I love you, Mom," Mike said looking at fallen tree. It was usually the first thing he said when he arrived. Mike waited as if the tree would speak back.

"I... wish you could see me now," Mike said. "Junior is six now. Dawn," he said, glancing at me, "is still putting up with me. I wish you could see it."

I tightened my grip naturally, wanting to console him. I thought of the girl in chains in my basement and loosened it again.

Mike's mother left him. She left his father when Mike was a young boy. She left Rick before he could say a full sentence.

She left her family.

Mike didn't talk to me about his mother for years. It was only after we got engaged that he opened up. One morning she said she had to leave while they were staying at the cabin. She never came home.

Mike was the same age as Junior at the time.

His father had to raise his two young children on his own. That made me think of Rick. It was much easier to understand the man he was when you found out about what his mother did to them.

The fallen tree was a place where Mike had fond memories of his mother. She would take him there, holding baby Rick in her arms as they hiked. She would sit on the tree stump and read to the boys, non-stop, for hours.

Mike loved his mother, even though he

struggled to remember her at times. At their last visit to the cabin, when he took Junior to visit his spot by the fallen tree, he admitted to me that he'd forgotten what her face looked like. He wept in front of his son that day.

I didn't understand. We had gone to his spot where he said he liked to visit his mother many times, but it was the first time he'd broke down in that way. Junior was more compassionate than me at that moment. He hugged his father and explained to me that he just missed his mommy. Junior had told me he would be sad too if he didn't have me.

That was when I started noticing Mike's change of behaviour. That was when he started leaving the house unexpectedly, mostly to be by himself, I suspected.

Mike touched the snow on top of the log and patted it with his hand.

"You know," he said, "sometimes I think about that day she left. My father was not the same. He was harder. Worse to be around than usual. Harold Vaughn and his wife, Anna. They were such a big help. Anna, she was like an angel. Brought food. A lot of food for my family." He lowered his head. "I only think about it because you saw him today. I feel bad for the old man."

"Do you want to visit him today?" I asked. I hoped he'd say yes. That would make it easier for me to ensure Amber got help and stayed safe.

"No," he answered curtly, but didn't elaborate.

I nodded and tightened my arm around him. I looked at the teardrop slowly making its way down his cheek. I brushed it away with my hand and he smiled at me.

I had never met Anna before her unfortunate passing. Mike had such praise for her. It was hard for me to believe the woman he talked about was in a union with the man I saw hiking behind the cabin today. Harold Vaughn seemed like anything but an angel, with the gun always over his shoulder.

"I'm sorry, Mom," Mike whispered, staring at the fallen tree.

"Why do you say that when we visit here?"

"I wish I could go back in time. I'd make a lot more better decisions. One of them would be to tell my mom how much I loved her before she left that day. Maybe she would have stayed. I don't know... Thanks for coming with me to visit her. It always means a lot to me."

"Of course," I said. Mike leaned in and closed his eyes. I took in a deep breath, thinking of Amber Townsin, locked in the butcher room. I closed my eyes and kissed him quickly.

"Okay," he said, opening his eyes. "Let's go into town."

CHAPTER 14

"I can drive," Mike said, taking out his keys from his jacket pocket.

Mike sat in the driver's seat and turned on the ignition, putting on the seat warmers immediately. I slowly sat in the passenger side.

"Is there anything better than heated seats? Starting to get cold outside," he said, shivering.

I looked at the large snowflakes coming down. The sun was beginning to set, and the forest becoming darker.

Amber Townsin needed me, I reminded myself.

Terry Shreb, my acting coach, was more than a mentor to me. I looked to him for life wisdom as well. He told me what to do when I questioned my acting skills. Play the part, Terry would say. Trick your audience into thinking you're not you. You may be scared on stage, worried that you'll forget lines and blow up a scene. None of that matters as much as this: does your audience find you authentic?

As Mike put the car in drive, I grabbed his

hand and held it tightly in his lap. It was something I'd done many times when we drove together.

I saw the smile on his face and knew he thought my act was authentic.

I was always good at lying when I had to. Acting came naturally.

The woman in the basement couldn't confirm who took her. The obvious answer was Mike. What were his intentions? If he did kidnap her, why was he so relaxed and acting normal? He knew I'd been in the basement as well. Was he hoping that somehow I hadn't noticed the woman downstairs?

Was Mike putting on a better performance than me?

Was he playing games?

Questions kill your performance. That was something Terry told me as well. Don't ask yourself the entire time if the audience likes you or hates you. You want the audience to find you authentic in your role, but you don't want to question yourself during your performance. Have a friend or someone you know will be honest with you take notes during the play. Ask them, how authentic did I come off? What you don't want to do is question anything you see an audience member do while you're on stage. If you see someone yawn in the crowd, it's not because they woke up at five in the morning, but because they find you boring. Don't do that to yourself.

Mike squeezed my hand, and I knew in my heart that he didn't know. What I wish I knew was the truth.

"Are you having a good birthday so far?" I asked him lovingly.

"Thanks for everything so far. It was definitely a good surprise."

I had a bad surprise, I thought to myself. "Good." Very soon I would have more of an audience. Sarah and Victor could come anytime. Sarah could be the member to give me notes, although it was a role I wish I never had to take.

Of course, I didn't want to add my friend to the situation. I looked out the window again at the snow.

"Maybe you're right about the weather," I said. "We could call Vic and Sarah, cancel with them for tonight. The last thing I want is for them to be upset about being snowed in. Besides, I don't mind being alone with the birthday boy."

Mike peered at me sidelong as he drove. He nodded slowly. "That works, sure." He stopped the car and put it in reverse. "We should go back to the cabin and call them. Cancel now."

I thought of Amber. Leaned forward eating dog food on the floor, with her hands cuffed behind her back.

"No, let's just go into town. We're already this far."

Mike put the car into drive again. When we

got to the main trail he turned and smiled at me.

"So, Lady MacBeth, are we practising your lines again tonight?" he asked.

It was touching that Mike cared so much about how my plays went. Ever since I joined the drama group in town, he's been nothing but supportive. He would be in the front row of anything I was in, even when I played the smallest of roles. He loved practising my lines. At night before going to sleep we would go through a scene together.

Although Mike could never get into his role as much as me, he loved watching me get into character. He called it magic. I think he enjoyed pretending to be on stage with me. He knew the lines enough that he could have been. Sometimes I caught him mouthing the lines from the front row.

"I think I got my role down solid now, thanks to you," I said. I smiled and he returned it.

How could such a man be the type to do something terrible to a woman like Amber? Mike squeezed my hand. He leaned over and kissed my cheek. I felt instant guilt.

I turned my head to the window, removing my hand from his lap. At that moment I spotted Harold's white truck parked on the edge of the road. In the driver's seat, Harold had his head down. When Mike's front lights illuminated him, he put a hand up to cover his face and waved.

Mike waved back and turned towards the

main road.

"What's he doing parked like that?" I asked.

"Who knows. The old man is squirrely now. Last time I saw him, he mistook me for my dad."

I laughed. "Your dad never wore glasses. I mean, when you take them off, sure I can see it, I guess."

Mike shook his head. "He's losing it. I can't imagine what it's like losing your wife. I'd probably go insane too."

Mike had told me the story of Harold's wife, Anna. It was tragic. A terrible accident. Mike had said it took days for the police to find her body.

"It was a boating accident, right?" I asked.

Mike shook his head. "Kayaking, so I guess you're kind of right. It happened right over here in Crescent Lake. His wife went out by herself. She was an avid kayaker. Harold said it was her idea to buy the cabin because it reminded her of being near the Great Lakes and all the water sports she did when she lived in Ontario. So that day, from what I understand, it was windy. The boat flipped underwater, and she wasn't able to roll herself back up."

"That happens all the time in kayaking, right?" I asked. "Shouldn't she have known how to turn herself back over?"

"Should have, yeah. You would think. Maybe she didn't have the strength? I don't know. Terrible, though. He found her in the water."

"I can't imagine," I said. I pictured him swimming to the kayak in front of the shore. Him putting his head under the water and seeing his wife's body. Her wide-eyed expression of fright permanently on her face.

I hated how visual my mind could be at times. Being an actor, I had a tendency to visualize terrible situations to get me to feel the emotions of others. It was a good trick if you wanted to feel a certain way before starting a scene.

Unfortunately for Harold Vaughn, it was his real life.

CHAPTER 15

The conversation was quiet until we were closer to town.

The sun was sinking low, casting a warm glow over the landscape. In the distance, the mountains rose up towards the sky, their peaks etched against the orange and pink. Suddenly, the sky was awash with deep red hues, as if a giant wound had opened up. The effect was eerie and unsettling. I began to feel claustrophobic in the car as the woods darkened more and more.

I concentrated on my breathing, without making it obvious to my husband. I glanced at him driving, and he stared at me with an expression of concern.

"Something wrong?" he asked.

I shook my head. "No, I was thinking about this scene in my play," I lied. "Lady Macbeth. It's hard to act crazy."

Mike grabbed my hand, and for a moment, my act slipped, tugging it away. I smiled at him and relaxed my fingers in his lap.

"I must have seen the sky like this a

thousand times, but it never gets old," Mike said.
I nodded in agreement. It was beautiful. It was as if an artist splashed colors into the air that didn't belong there. Mike and I would sometimes sit on the bench outside the cabin and watch the sun completely set behind the mountains. It was beautiful – usually.

Tonight, it was menacing. A woman was tied up in the cabin. Her life depended on me. The colors in the sky were a reminder of the blood that would be spilt if I did nothing.

He might not have intended to kill her, I thought. Did he intend to abuse her? Hurt her? What would Mike have done had I not surprised him with a last-minute trip to the cabin?

It's not him, a voice called out from inside me. It was the part of me that had been married to him for thirteen years. It was the woman who shared a child with him. It was the side of me that tried to remind myself that he was a good father. A loving husband.

Sure, he's been acting weird lately. Leaving at night when Junior goes to bed. Coming back late, and not giving me a lot of answers. Many wives would assume their husbands would be cheating on them, but I never worried about that too much. Mike was not that kind of man I thought.

"I went out for a late movie," Mike would say sometimes. How many movies could come out in one week, though?

Mike didn't drink heavily as far as I knew, but sometimes he said he would be going to meet up with Rick at the bar.

I turned my head slightly and from the corner of my eye, watched Mike drive. He bobbed his head to an old rock song.

He used to be a loving husband.

Who is he now?

A man who kidnapped a young woman.

What will happen when the police show up at our cabin? When they arrest Mike? Junior will someday see the news. Hell, he's old enough to Google it already.

It's not him, a voice said inside me again. It was as if my heart and my head were having a tug-o-war inside me.

Who else could it be if not Mike? The most logical answer was that my husband kidnapped the girl. Amber Townsin, I reminded myself. That was her name. Calling her anything else dehumanized her.

We passed a sign. "Town of Canmore. Population 15,990."

Located near the popular tourist spot of Banff, Alberta, Canmore was overshadowed at times by the crowds who visited internationally. That was usually fine by me. Less crowded the better.

After the song finished, a DJ came on with a somber voice. "Next up we have Metallica. Before we continue, I have to share some news that's not very upbeat, but important to share. The Royal Canadian Mounted Police have issued a missing person report for a woman named Amber Townsin. You can find a picture of her on our website. The police have concerns for her safety, and if you have any information about her disappearance please contact 911 immediately. Her name again is Amber Townsin. She was last seen at—"

Mike turned the channel abruptly. "I hate Metallica," he said with a grunt. He stopped when he heard the voice of Justin Bieber. It was a song that had been popular on the radio lately, playing every twenty minutes at least, but I could never remember the words. Mike started banging his head harder than he did to the rock song, saying every word. He grinned at me but stopped when he saw my expression of fear.

"What?" he asked.

I closed my mouth and got back into the character of the sweet, trusting wife. "Your head banging to a Justin Bieber song is the scariest thing I've ever seen."

He raised the volume and banged his head harder to the beat.

"Okay, okay," I said with a chuckle. "Watch the road. You're hugging the curb."

He rolled his eyes. "My driving is perfect. Your driving is the scariest thing I've ever experienced." He laughed at his joke.

I smiled but felt my stomach turn. He changed the channel on the radio when they mentioned Amber's disappearance. Worse, was how... happy he was. You couldn't get more than a smile from him the past few months. Suddenly he had more energy and a sense of humor.

"What do you think of Vic?" he asked.

"What?" I said, confused.

Mike turned down the radio. "Vic? Victor. What do you think of him?"

I shrugged. "Sarah only tells me good things. You two seemed to hit it off well. When he told me he used to hunt as a kid with his father, I knew you two would have some stories to share. Why do you ask?"

"I don't know. He's a good guy. Maybe he just had a bit too much to drink last time."

I was authentically surprised at that. "I had no clue you two hung out together outside of our couple dates. You never told me."

"Yeah. Last week. He texted me. Said he wanted to get together for some fishing. I took him to Crescent Lake, and the cabin."

"You took Vic to the cabin before?" I said, still shocked. As far as I knew, Mike didn't even have Victor's phone number. "Why didn't you tell me?"

"I don't know. Well—"

"Sarah didn't even tell me," I said. "I'm surprised she wouldn't have mentioned it at work."

"Sarah didn't know either," Mike said,

staring at me with a smirk.

"What? Why wouldn't he tell his wife?" I smacked him on the shoulder. "Why wouldn't you tell your wife either?"

"He said he got into it pretty well with Sarah. Some stupid fight. He didn't really tell me much about what happened."

"So, why are you telling me about it now?"

Mike shrugged. "I just... got the feeling he's seeing someone else besides Sarah."

I gasped, unable to hold back how I felt. "Vic? No way. Sarah and he seem so good together."

"That's how I felt too. We both had a bit too much beer that day."

"Wait, what day was this?"

"I took Thursday off last week. I met up with him at the cabin. I thought he could use some, what do they call it, 'bro time'."

I nodded but couldn't control my thoughts. How many days does Mike take off and not tell me? How many visits to the cabin does he have without me?

"So why do you feel he's talking to another woman?" I asked.

"Could be nothing." Mike stopped at an intersection. He turned to me. "When he drinks, I mean, when he's drunk, he's very different. The way he talked about Sarah... it took me back."

"What did he say?"

He shook his head. "I... don't want to get into

that. Anyways, he was trying to show me a pic on his cell of a truck he's looking at to buy, but the first photo that popped up was a young woman. She looked straight out of high school. It was weird. Okay, I'll say it, the girl had her large breasts out."

"A woman sent him a topless picture?"

"That's what I think. I asked him who she was, and he just made this weird face and quickly changed the photo to the truck."

I stared blankly out the window. I wondered if Sarah had any indication. Should I say anything to her?

"I don't know," Mike continued. "That girl on his phone. The way he talked about Sarah, and just women in general. It was worse than Rick, I tell you."

"How's that possible?"

The light changed to green. Mike turned away from me. "I don't know, Vic comes off like a player to me. I don't know if I want to be friends like that with him. Maybe it's better we just do couple things together and not one-to-one." Mike laughed. "While we were at the cabin, he saw that fake rock thing we keep our extra key in, in case we got locked out. He pointed it out right away. I think we need to find a new place to hide the key."

CHAPTER 16

When we arrived at the grocery store in town, Mike parked in the nearly empty lot. He stepped out of the car and stretched.

"You want to grab the veggies?" he asked. "I'll grab the meat and chips."

Mike could never take his time with anything. He seemed to enjoy pretending whatever he was doing was like a pit stop at the Indie 500. He wanted to complete the task as fast as those crews put on tires, and always wanted to have a plan on how to do it.

Divide and conquer, as he would say.

"We should get everything quickly," he said. "Get back to the cabin and call Sarah and cancel with them. Divide and conquer," he said on cue.

I smiled. He had suggested exactly what I knew he would. I used to think Mike could never surprise me with his actions. Amber Townsin changed everything. The voices inside my head continued to fight with each other on what was happening.

Then I spotted the payphone outside the

grocery store. My smile grew wider. I'd completely forgotten about it. The phonebooth looked like it was straight out of the 90's.

At that moment it didn't matter if Mike had kidnapped Amber or not, what mattered was me getting her help.

"Divide and conquer," I repeated, swinging my hand.

I walked into the small-town grocery store, my boots squeaking on the linoleum floor. The bell above the door chimed as we entered, alerting the cashier to our presence. The store was quiet, with only a few other customers milling about, their carts filled with various items. The store was cramped and cluttered, with boxes and bags of merchandise stacked haphazardly in every available space.

Mike gave me a quarter for my cart. He got his own.

"Meet you at the till?" he asked, in more of a demanding way, and I nodded.

He watched me until I headed towards the produce area. When I was close to the lettuce, I turned, and he brushed past me. I watched him walk down an aisle towards the meat section. When he was out of sight, I looked outside the window at the payphone.

I grabbed a few items, putting them in the cart. When I was certain Mike was out of sight, I walked back to the front of the store, leaving my cart near a cashier. I quickly ran through a line, pushing past an old man wearing a grey vest who was about to pay. I apologized without looking back at him.

When I was outside, I nearly ran to the payphone. I shoved the push door and closed it hard behind me. The sign above the phone said it cost a quarter to use and I let out a heavy sigh.

I had not brought my purse.

I glanced around but nobody was nearby. I stared through the phone booth's dirt-stained glass at the grocery store and at the cashier inside. Faster than before, I ran back into the store, and nearly struck the old man at the counter again. He grunted at me.

I raised my hands in surrender. "Sorry," I said to him. He shook his head, as if to say, people these days.

I turned to the cashier. "Can I get a quarter please?"

"We don't give out money for carts, ma'am," she said.

"It's not for a cart... Whatever." I was about to grab my cart for the quarter when I saw Mike passing an aisle. He turned his head in my direction before disappearing again. "I just really need a quarter please."

The woman at the cash register rolled her eyes at me. "I can't just give you money, miss."

"Take mine," the old man said, taking out

his wallet. He opened up a small pouch inside and took out a shiny coin. "Now, please, respect your elders. Whatever rush you are in, it's not okay to knock into people like that." His face crinkled as he smiled, but he didn't lower the coin to my hand. "Whatever your hurry is, just remember it's not life or death. You learn these things as you get older."

I looked around for Mike. "Yes, you're right. Sorry, it's just an emergency."

"Alright. No problem," he said, dropping the coin in my hand.

"Thank you!" I said, beaming. I quickly but softly went past the man, and ran to the booth.

I picked up the receiver, dropping the coin in the slot. I placed the phone to my ear and dialed 911.

Nothing happened. I dialled 911 again. There were no sounds from the phone. I slammed the phone down, and it fell, hanging. When I went to push the door, I saw the ripped sign taped to it.

"Out of Order."

I rolled my eyes.

"What are you doing?" I turned to find Mike staring at me curiously. The cart he had was full and included the few items I had grabbed when I was in the store. "Why are you trying to use a broken phone?" He pointed at the sign. "That's a very Dawn thing to do," he said, laughing. "Who were you going to call?"

I tried to hide my shock and frustration.

"Junior," I lied.

"We just spoke with him," Mike said with a smirk.

"I know, but sometimes I get... worried. Mother's intuition."

Mike shook his head. "He's with your mom. Let's go to the liquor store and head back to the cabin. We can put aside our no phones rule for you to call him. I wouldn't mind talking to him. It's funny how guilty I feel when we're going to have a fun weekend and he's not with us." He opened the trunk with his key fob and rolled the cart up to it.

"You coming?" he asked when I didn't follow. I reluctantly did. Part of me felt like running back inside the store and screaming for help. What would Mike do if I did?

He would likely be so confused. Would he leave? Run to the car and take off? Would he stop at the cabin for Amber? Dispose of the evidence?

I smiled at Mike, trying my best not to let my worries show. "Liquor store sounds good. Sarah and I need a few bottles of wine too."

All of the beer was kept in the cooler in the back. I could make my move then. Call the cops using the cashier's phone. Explain it's an emergency. Tell him not to say anything to my husband. Pretend I'm talking to Junior if I had to. It would be easy enough to act like a concerned mother. Give the cops my name, the address of the cabin right away. Tell them Amber's Townsin is there. The cops were already looking for her.

I got back inside the car. Mike closed the trunk and pushed the cart back. He quickly turned on the ignition and warmed his hands over the heating vent.

He turned out of the parking lot towards the chain mall that had the liquor store, but passed it.

"What are you doing?" I asked. "Did you forget where the beer store is?" I laughed, trying to keep my cool.

He laughed back. "I don't know. What happened with Vic bothered me. I think it's better that we don't drink this weekend. My gut tells me that's a bad idea. I could say something to Victor. What if he makes a comment towards you? I wouldn't be able to handle that. Our couples dates would end disastrously. It's better we don't drink."

"Sarah and I would like to!" I said loudly.

"Well, too bad," Mike said. "If I can't drink, nobody gets to." He saw how frustrated I was and softened his face. "Trust me, it's better this way. I'd rather us just have fun. It's my birthday request."

CHAPTER 17

Amber

My sense of time in the basement was all messed up. No windows. No way to tell if it was day or night. No way to tell how long I had truly been there for.

When the door closed upstairs and I heard no further movement, I waited for what felt like forever before I made a sound. "Help," I said to myself at first. It was as if I'd forgotten how to use my voice.

My attempts at lubricating my hands with the water to squeeze the handcuffs off had been fruitless, and stupid. Of course, I couldn't get free of them. How out of touch was I?

The throbbing in my head was still present but less invasive. I could think more clearly.

My thoughts had come to the same conclusion. I can't escape.

I stood up from the cold cement floor, attempting to grab the fallen chair with my hands behind my back. It took some time, but I managed to turn the chair over and back to where it had been. I sat and lowered my head.

Why me? I thought. What could be the reason something this... terrible would happen to me? What had I done to the universe that would allow me to wake up in this man's basement?
I thought of the man with the wolf head. No doubt he would come back, and soon.

Would Dawn be able to do something before the man in the wolf mask came back?

I thought of the mask. The wolf's menacing face.

"Help!" I screamed. I stood up and took a deep breath. I wouldn't wind up like those women you heard about in true crime stories. All of them probably knew they were doomed. How many of those women fought with every inch of their soul? How many thought their capture would let them live?

I had been at my lowest when Dawn found me. Part of me had wanted this to end. I had wished it was the man in the mask, so he could end my suffering.

Not now. I would do whatever it took. Fight with everything I had. This man would not have an easy victim.

He thinks he's a wolf. He believes I'm his prey.

He wanted me to be quiet. I knew that meant there was a chance someone could hear me. He said he would kill me if I shouted. So what? What was he planning on doing with me anyway?

Death was the inevitable outcome of my situation. It didn't take a law school mind to realize that.

"Help!" I shouted louder. "Help! Help me! I'm Amber Townsin! I've been kidnapped! Help me!"

The front door opened, and a single set of footsteps crossed the room upstairs. I knew before I heard them coming down the stairs that it was him.

"Help me!" I screamed. "He's going to kill me! Help! My name is Amber—"

The door opened and the man with the wolf head stepped inside, staring at me with the cold eyes of his mask. He was even more menacing than I remembered.

"Your name is Amber Townsin," he said with a deep voice. "I know. I've heard about it on the radio too." He raised his head to the ceiling. "Help! Help! Help me!" he shouted in a higher pitch, mocking me. He laughed and tilted his head back, howling like the wolf he was.

I picked up the metal chair and held the top firmly in my hands. He stepped closer and I spun around with the chair, attempting to strike him. He stepped back easily and laughed again.

"I told you to stay quiet," he said with a deep voice. "I told you I'd put you down like the dog you were if you tried anything. It looks like you tried. I heard you shouting, many times. You've been a bad little bitch. Now I'll put you down."

This was the part where I was supposed to be scared. Instead, it enraged me further. "Fuck you!" I shouted back. He took a step closer to me and I swung the chair harder. Again, he easily dodged my attempt.

He stepped outside the room and came back holding a rifle. He pointed it at my chest.

"You don't listen so well," he said. "You forgot to call me 'Master'. You don't remember your place. You haven't listened to any of the rules."

I breathed in deep and turned my body, throwing the chair at him. This time it struck him, causing him to lose focus with the rifle. I ran towards him, but the chain stopped me several inches from hitting him. I turned, attempting to grab the rifle with my hands.

He raised his leg and booted me to the floor. My forehead struck the cement and I cried out in pain.

The man with the wolf mask laughed again. "I enjoy you; I do. We never got to have fun together. Something tells me you were never going to play nice, though. It's better we end this before we have unwelcome visitors again. Now, go up against the wall, your hands facing me."

"No!" I shouted, struggling to find my balance as I stood up. I straightened my back and raised my head at him. "You're a rapist, murderous, misogynist piece of shit. You think you're a predator, a wolf. You're a joke! You think you're above women?" I shook my head with a grin. "You're nothing but a loser. You're not a master. You're a fucking peasant."

The man in the wolf's mask stared at me in response. I waited for him to be enraged. Yell back. Curse me. Strike me even. Instead, he watched me for several seconds. My face dropped when he continued to make no movement for what felt like an eternity.

Without warning he raised the rifle and pulled the trigger.

CHAPTER 18

Dawn

The ride back to the cabin was tense and filled with fear, at least for me, and not that I showed it. I held Mike's hand in his lap, and he drove along the wooded dirt road.

Mike broke the silence. "I want to thank you," he said, taking a quick moment to squeeze my hand. "It's really nice, you wanting to surprise me like this. I don't appreciate how amazing you are, and I should show it more."

I squeezed his hand in return, trying to hide the terror that was consuming me. "I wanted to do something special."

Mike smiled, completely unaware of the nightmare I was living through. "Well, it was a surprise."

I smiled back. This weekend was most certainly a surprise. A nightmare really. I tried my best to continue to act as close to normal as I could. All I wanted to do since coming to the cabin and finding... her, was to run away, into the forest.

Away from Mike. Away from Amber even.

My life wasn't perfect before I found her, but it made... sense. Finding her in the basement changed everything. Sure, I'd done a good job of charming my husband, but I was scared. What had he done to the young woman? What was he planning to do to her? Would he do something to me?

What was he planning to do with us? If he put her in the basement, he would know that eventually she could try and yell and scream.

Was he hoping the girl would stay quiet long enough to come up with a plan to get rid of her?

My soul felt crushed thinking that the man I loved would do something like that to another woman. That was not who Mike was, or at least who I thought he was.

Mike turned right onto the trail leading to our cabin. It wouldn't be long now until we were back. What should I do?

Amber's Townsin was handcuffed to a chain in our basement, and I felt like there was nothing I could do about it.

I raised an eyebrow and turned my head. A key. There had to be a key for the handcuffs somewhere in the house. Perhaps Amber had an idea where Mike put them.

Did Amber see where her captor kept the key? Did he keep it on him? Mike carried a group of keys on his keychain. I had made fun of him calling him a janitor with his collection.

Mike had a tendency to keep his keys in his jacket pocket at home. I could find a way to grab them and check. What did a handcuff key even look like? I sighed.

“Are you mad at me?” Mike asked.

I turned to him and faked a smile. “Why would I be?”

“You’re usually the chatty one.”

“Bad day at work,” I lied.

“Your boss again? What's that prick's name?”

“Ronald,” I answered. “Not him. It’s hard dealing with bad calls from customers all day. It’s starting to get to me, I guess.”

He nodded. “Quit. You don’t need to put up with anything in life that's bothering you this much. Focus on your acting.”

Today was a masterclass in how to not act scared shitless. I’d thought I was doing a good job until Mike commented on how weird I was being. Amber was relying on me to help her. I couldn’t let her down again.

I had to find a way to get the cuffs off her. Then I could get the car keys and take off with Amber in the backseat. I thought about how I could sneak around and search for a key.

There was also a gun in the house to worry about now. I smiled when I realized Mike likely didn't have any ammo. As far as I remembered, Rick hadn't given him any.

Mike slowed down as he neared the cabin. When he was near a complete stop, I opened the car door. "I have to go to the bathroom badly!" I shouted and ran to the cabin. I wanted to run down and speak with Amber. I needed info on where the key could be for the cuffs.

Mike grinned as I ran to the front door and hauled on it; I'd forgotten he locked it. I yelled at him to throw me the keys. He laughed and tossed them over. Thankfully the car lights illuminated the keys flying through the air. I somehow managed to catch them and unlocked the door.

"Thanks for shutting your door!" Mike called out playfully, as I ran inside. I closed the door behind me. Out the window, I saw Mike taking his time walking round to the trunk. Despite moving slowly, I realized I didn't have enough time to get downstairs before he'd come inside.

I locked the front door.

I couldn't let him in. Now was the time to make my stand. The phones were above the fridge. Amber Townsin couldn't wait for me any longer to help her. The gun was still on the table.

I didn't have time to search for handcuff keys, while Amber relieved herself in a bucket in my basement, scared for her life. I should have tried harder in town to get help.

Now was my time to do something.

I ran to the fridge, jumped and grabbed the

cellphones. To my surprise there was only one: mine. I had thought Mike put his back above the fridge after speaking with Junior. Did he have his phone on him the whole time we were in town?

There was no time to waste thinking about it. I opened my phone and ran down the stairs, nearly tripping on the narrow steps.

What would Mike do after I called the cops? I thought. Would he try and break in? Hurt Amber, or me? It could take some time for the cops to get to the cabin. How could we remain safe while waiting for the cops to arrive?

I unlocked the deadbolt and opened the door to the butcher room, dialing 911 with my other hand.

I smiled, anticipating Amber's reaction when she saw I had a phone in my hand calling for help.

My smile vanished quickly when I looked inside. My mouth gaped open.

Nothing. There was nothing in the room. The chain was gone. The handcuffs too. The metal chair was up against the wall.

Amber Townsin was missing.

CHAPTER 19

The dog food scattered across the floor had been cleaned up and the bowls removed. Even the bucket was missing.

The pounding on the front door distracted me. "Hey!" Mike shouted. "The door is locked. Let me in!" His voice was muffled, but I could clearly hear him. "Dawn, the door is locked! It's cold outside! Hurry up in the bathroom, come on!"

He continued to knock harder and harder, but I was unable to react. Instead, all I could do was stare at the empty room where Amber had been. I slowly left and closed the door behind me.

"Let me in," Mike shouted from outside.

The phone in my hand vibrated. It was Mike. He does have his phone on him, I thought. I declined the call.

I walked up the stairs slowly, trying to understand what was happening. Was I going crazy? Had I imagined everything? It was as if I was becoming as unsettled as Lady Macbeth in my play.

"What are you doing?" Mike shouted. "Let! Me! In!" He pounded on the door, emphasizing every word.

When I reached the top of the stairs, the knocking and yelling stopped. Instead of Mike's anger, I heard laughter.

"Vic, Sarah!" he shouted.

I breathed in deep. Our guests had arrived. The friends I was supposed to call and cancel with.

I continued to hear them talk outside. I opened the door slowly and Sarah smiled at me. Vic was hugging Mike. At my feet were the grocery bags Mike had left at the door. Sarah's smile waned as she waited for my usual happy response to seeing her.

"What's wrong?" she asked.

I couldn't find the words this time. I couldn't seem happy. I couldn't act my way out of this. "Hey, Sarah," I said in a somber tone.

"Is everything okay?"

Mike seemed happier than ever. Vic wrapped his arm around his shoulder and whispered something in his ear. My husband belly laughed at whatever he said.

"Of course," I lied. "We were waiting for you two to come." I spotted there were two extra vehicles beside ours. "You guys took two cars here?"

"Vic thought he was going to be stuck at work even longer so I said I would meet him here."

"And," Victor said, raising a finger, "I still beat her here by thirty minutes!" He looked at Mike. "She's really good at driving to the speed limit."

Sarah rolled her eyes in response. "Well,

we're both here now, and we can't wait for this weekend."

"This will be one for the books." Vic laughed. "Snowed in with the Nelsons."

"Yeah, looks like," Mike said, eyeing the snow falling around us. "Come on inside, guys."

Mike walked up the steps and patted me on the shoulder. "You made me scared. I was waiting outside. I thought I was going to be an ice cube by the time you came back."

I laughed, reluctantly. "I... must have locked the door for some reason when I ran inside, sorry."

Mike smiled. I still had the phone in my hand with 911 dialed, but I didn't hit the call button. I didn't understand what was happening.

Heavy snow was coming down furiously. The landscape was quickly being blanketed in a layer of white, the trees around us disappearing beneath the snowy veil.

"Okay, let's catch up inside," Vic said with his usual aggressive tone. "My balls are frozen."

The four of us went indoors. Mike grabbed the groceries and Vic slammed the door behind us. Mike saw the phone in my hand and quickly grabbed it.

"You know the rules." Mike turned to Vic and Sarah. "We have a rule at the cabin: no phones. They're too distracting. We come out here to get away from the world of social media, news headlines, or anything else."

"Good idea," Sarah said. "Here, take mine." She grabbed her cell phone out of her pocket and gave it to him.

Victor glanced at her. "Really, Sarah? Are you going to be able to tear yourself away from your phone the whole weekend?"

Sarah shook her head playfully. "I'm not the one who can't go number two in the bathroom without their cell."

"Okay, okay. Now you're giving TMI to our friends."

"It's just something Dawn and I do," Mike said to Vic. "You can keep yours."

Victor sighed. "I'll agree to your rules." He slid his hand into his pocket and outstretched his cell phone to Mike, who put them all on top of the fridge. He reached into his jacket pocket, took out his own and looked at me for a moment before adding it to the top of the fridge.

"Wait..." He turned to me. "You wanted to talk to Junior again, right?" He grabbed his phone and held it in front of me.

Before I could answer or snap out of my daze, Vic waved his hand. "Don't worry about the little man. He's fine. You're just having mother's guilt for wanting to have fun. Now, let's drink and... have fun. Happy birthday, buddy," Vic said again, embracing Mike with a heavy hug.

Although Victor initially came across as sly and arrogant, there were moments when his true personality shone through. Despite his tough exterior, there was a softer side to him as well. He had a quick wit and a sharp sense of humor and was always the life of the party when he was with his friends. Sarah had told me they met at a university party. Vic, go figure, was one of the frat boys who hosted it.

"The big four-oh-no," he said.

Mike put his phone on top of the fridge. "Stop reminding me. Dawn has done a good job reminding me all day of how old I am. But I have a better question for everyone here," Mike said with a grin. "Who's up for a fun night?"

CHAPTER 20

"What's the plan? What's the birthday boy thinking of doing tonight?" Vic asked, his voice dripping with excitement. "Strippers, shots, dance party?"

"Board games," Mike replied nonchalantly.

"Boring games," Vic repeated, earning a slap on the shoulder from Sarah.

"You love playing board games with Dawn and Mike," she said. "Don't even pretend."

"I love playing games more when I have a drink in me." Vic eyed Mike expectantly. "What do you have on tap here?"

"Sorry. We don't have any beer."

"No beer!" Vic said in horror. "Isn't that the whole point of camping out in the woods?"

Mike laughed. "I'm an old man now, Vic. Don't you remember? Drinking is for you young tykes. Would water be okay?"

Vic sighed. "Of course."

I finally snapped out of it and put on a happy face. "We have steak for you guys. I can start cooking before the games."

"Now we're talking," he said with a grin.

Sarah smiled at me. "I can help you cook."

That was exactly what I was hoping for.

I waved to Sarah, and we headed to the kitchen. The room was small and cozy, with a gas range stove in the corner and a wooden table in the center. The walls were adorned with pictures of our past visits with Junior.

I realized the only right decision I had made this weekend was not bringing him on this trip.

As I prepared the meal, Sarah continued to watch me curiously. I grabbed the meat from the fridge, then took my cast iron skillet from a cabinet and placed it on the stove.

"Are you sure everything's okay?" she asked.

It wasn't. No, nothing was okay. Amber Townsin was missing. My husband had taken her and now she was not where I found her. The voice inside me yelled at me to make more sense of my situation. If Mike had kidnapped Amber, then who let her go while we were away? Something else was happening here, and I didn't understand it.

I looked back at Vic, who was talking jovially to my husband. Victor had arrived in his own car before Sarah. Thirty minutes, he said. I remembered what Mike said about him on the drive into town.

He accused him of cheating on Sarah and being nasty towards women in general. I knew Vic to be smug at times, arrogant at his worst, but he had never made any negative comments towards me. Whatever he said to Mike was enough for him not to want to get alcohol.

Thirty minutes later, he was alone near the cabin.

What if Victor was the one who took Amber? Thirty minutes was enough to get her out of the basement and clean up. But where was she? If Vic was the one who moved her, where would he have brought her in such a short time? And how did Victor know we would be out of the house to grab Amber?

I suddenly remembered Mike had his phone on him when we had left town. The whole time I said I wanted to call Vic and Sarah to cancel, I said I wanted to call Junior, and he had a phone on him? He said he didn't realize he still had it. My husband, someone obsessed with attention to detail, forgot his cell phone was in his pocket when I said I wanted to call Sarah and our son.

What if my husband and Victor had worked together on kidnapping Amber?

"Everything's okay," I lied, trying to shake off my suspicions. "So, did you have a hard time getting to the cabin by yourself?"

Sarah shook her head. "Not really. I texted Vic when I was close, and he waited for me by the highway."

I nodded. "That's weird how he got here before you."

Sarah smirked. “Vic does continuously like to make fun of my driving. I ride the break, he likes to say. With the snow falling, I took my time. I need new tires.”

That’s when I thought of the answer. The car. Where else could Amber Townsin be? She could be in the trunk right now, freezing to death.

Was there a way I could check without making it obvious? Should I say something to Sarah? At this moment, she was the only one I could trust.

I lowered my head. “I was really looking forward to this weekend,” I said, “but something happened.”

Sarah had removed the wrapping from the meat and put it on the cutting board. She was mid salting it when I said the words and she stopped in her tracks.

"What do you mean?" she asked. "Did Mike say something to you? Do you know? You weren't supposed to know.” She shook her head. “Now the weekend is ruined.”

My mouth dropped. “You know about her?” I asked, stunned.

“Who’s *she*?” Sarah said, her brow furrowed. “Wait, are you saying Mike was with someone else?”

I shook my head. “The woman in the basement. Amber. I found her.”

“Amber?” Sarah said. She smiled. “What are

you saying here, Dawn? I'm so confused."

"We went out into town to grab a few things for the weekend. When we came back, she wasn't there."

I glanced back at Mike, who was still speaking to Victor and laughing about something. Mike brushed past us and grabbed the gun that was still on the table. He brought it back to Victor and handed it to him.

"Mike, we should test out your new gift," Vic said. "Let's shoot some rounds outside."

"I've got some ammo in the car that Rick gave me. Not sure we should, though."

Vic laughed. "Why not? Who's going to complain? You don't have too many neighbors around here, I take it."

"One that's not too far. Harold Vaughn. That old man is likely to join in, though, instead of reporting us."

"So is that a yes?"

"I suppose," Mike said with a grin.

"Hell yeah. Bang," Vic said, imitating a shot. He aimed the gun around the room playfully and pointed it at Sarah.

I turned back to her, not amused with her husband's antics.

Sarah chuckled uncomfortably. "This is, what, part of your lines for your play or something?"

I shook my head, trying to keep my voice

calm and not say my words too loudly. Before I could continue Mike walked up behind me and grabbed my shoulders, massaging my back.

"Hey," he said, kissing the back of my neck. "I can't remember where we put the board games. Maybe we can play Clue tonight." When he noticed the shock in Sarah's face, he looked at me, concerned.

Sarah's mouth still gaped open from what I had said.

"Your wife is something," she said. "Go ahead. Tell him the lines that you just told me."

I stared at Mike, not knowing what to do.

"Go ahead, tell him what you just told me," she said. "You're not going to believe how good your wife is at acting. She literally scared me with her intensity. This must be for that horror project you were telling me about at the Playhouse. You want to play the bad guy, right? *Misery*, the play. Gosh, you are something else."

I smiled back at Mike. "My husband already knows how good I am at acting."

"Yep, she's been putting up with me her whole life and pretending she loves it." He laughed, and Sarah did too. Vic was still pointing the gun around the room behind us.

I continued to prepare the steak. I watched out the window above the sink as the snow continued to fly down.

Where was Amber Townsin?

CHAPTER 21

Sarah made the table and the men sat down as she plated with their food and brought it to them.

"Thanks," Vic said. He glanced at his plate and cut a piece of steak. He put it in his mouth and sat back in his chair, shaking his head. "Whoa. This is the best steak I've had."

Mike smiled. "I picked the cut. Dawn knows how to cook it the way I like."

"I'm not joking, guys. This is the best steak I've had." Vic swallowed. "The only atrocity of this situation is the fact that I don't have a beer to wash this down with."

It was the third or fourth comment Vic had made since coming to the cabin about the lack of alcohol. And it surely wouldn't be the last.

Sarah slapped him on the shoulder again. "You need to wait for everyone to have their plate before you start eating. What kind of a barbarian are you?"

Vic sneered at her. "Whatever."

Mike just made a face. "Thank you for the

compliment, Vic."

I sat down at the other side of the table from Mike, watching everyone eat. No one seemed to have a care in the world as they continued to talk. Mike and Vic continued their conversation about his new gun.

"It was my father's rifle," Mike said. "He used it all the time when he went hunting with me and Rick."

"How is Rick?"

"He's doing okay."

"It's been a long time since I've seen him." Victor took another bite, and I stared at him. I wasn't aware that Vic even knew Rick, besides the stories Mike told at our couples dates. Then again, there wasn't a lot I knew about when it came to Vic and Mike's relationship outside of me and Sarah.

"He's doing okay," Mike repeated. "I wish he would find somebody though."

"Your brother doesn't seem like the type to settle down."

"That's certainly true," Mike said. "He just needs to find the right woman I guess." Mike glanced at me and back at Vic.

"So, when do we go hunting?" Vic asked, eyeing the weapon that was now on the couch.

"I don't hunt anymore. It's been years."

"Why not? I can see you're not a vegetarian," he said as Mike forked a huge piece of steak into his mouth.

"That is certainly true too. I lost the spirit of hunting a long time ago."

"What are you going to do with the gun if you're not going to hunt with it?"

Mike shrugged. "Go to the shooting range maybe."

"Where will you keep it? You'll have to buy a gun safe for your home."

"I'm thinking of just renting a locker at a gun range and keeping it there." He looked at me. "I don't really want to keep it in the house, you know, because of Junior."

Sarah nodded. "Well, boys and their toys. I wouldn't want a gun in my house." She stared at Victor intensely.

"What? We don't have kids. Why would you care? Scared I'd use it on you?" He laughed, but Sarah rolled her eyes and ate another piece of steak.

"Next month is your anniversary, right?" she asked me to change the subject.

Mike answered for me. "That's right."

"How many years now?"

"Fourteen years," I said in a low voice, staring at my husband. Most of them were happy, I thought. They were filled with as much love as a woman could ask for. When Junior was born, our home was even brighter. All of that changed when I found Amber Townsin.

Vic nodded and finished his last bit of steak. "Well done." He turned to Mike. "How does she not drive you crazy after so long?" Sarah again rolled her eyes.

Mike glanced at me, as if to say, 'this is what I mean about Vic', before replying. "You find the things you love about each other and focus on that. Don't stay angry at each other for too long, if you can." He shrugged. "When you get really angry, remind yourself why you married them to begin with."

Sarah smiled. "That's sweet, Mike. I always loved the story about how you two met. Vic never heard it. Dawn, tell him the story. You're so full of expression with your stories."

I turned away. I didn't want to look at my husband. I usually loved to tell it and would take any opportunity to do so. I was even certain that I had told it to Victor and Sarah before.

I couldn't tell it now. All I could think about was Amber. What Mike might have done to her. Where was she now? Maybe she escaped? Where would she have run to if she had?

I knew that wasn't likely though. Why would she clean up the dog food before running for her life?

Outside the window, Victor's car was barely visible in the snowfall.

"I told you how we met before," I said to Sarah.

"Victor hasn't heard it. Oh, c'mon."

"I can do it," Mike said, taking a sip of water.

"I've heard Dawn say it so many times to people, I'm sure I can muster her storytelling abilities just once... I was twenty-seven years old. We were here, at the cabin, with my father. It was a steaming hot summer day and Rick and I went down to Crescent Lake for a swim. Usually, the place was deserted. That day was different." Mike stared at me with a smile. "A group of young girls in their bikinis were jumping in the water, except one, who was tanning by herself."

"I like where this story is going already," Victor said. Again, Sarah rolled her eyes at him. It was as if Victor was attempting to win the grand prize for how much he could annoy his wife in one weekend.

"By the time Rick and I got to the lake, the girls were packing up, except... well, you know who." He waved a hand at me. "Dawn was the girl tanning. Her friends wanted to leave and go back to the cottage that they rented. Dawn said she didn't even have a chance to swim yet. So, her friends actually left her by herself, while they started bringing everything back to their car. Dawn stood up, showing off her tanned body, and right away, I was already in love." Mike laughed, and so did Vic.

I shook my head. That wasn't how I would usually tell the story.

"Anyway," he continued, "most people like to step into the water from the shore, but many jump off from the dock. It can be pretty deep, though.

Dawn, not so good at swimming. She stood at the end of the dock and looked around, and that was when she noticed me."

"Caught you gawking at her was more like it," Vic laughed.

Mike smirked. "I tried not to make it obvious, but she was beautiful." Mike stared at me again, and I quickly turned away. "Dawn finally jumped into the water. Huge splash. And... nothing."

"Nothing?" Vic repeated, not understanding.

"She didn't come back up. I was waiting for this beauty to emerge from the lake, but we didn't see her. After a minute I looked at Rick, who shared the same expression of concern I had. Where did she go? I was the first to take off my shirt and run to the end of the dock. Rick followed. I jumped into the water and found Dawn right away."

"What happened?"

"Cardiac arrest," Mike said, pursing his lips. "The cold water, after sitting out in the sun, was too much for her body."

"That can happen?" Vic said, surprised.

Mike nodded. "She was having a heart attack in the water. Rick helped me pull her out onto the dock, and he ran to get her friends and get help. I stayed with her. I calmed her until paramedics came. And the next day I went to the hospital where Dawn was recovering. I left a card by her bedside, wishing her a good recovery. Dawn was sleeping. I didn't even talk to her."

Mike turned to me, and this time I stared back at him. His soft brown eyes looked at me with love in them. I wish I could have returned the expression, but I couldn't. I couldn't pretend anymore.

"So how did you two hook up after?"

"My mother-in-law." Mike laughed. "When I brought the card, she and Dawn's father were already there. She asked who I was. I told her how I found Dawn in the lake. She called me her hero, and asked for my number, so Dawn could thank me when she was up to it. When she did call," Mike said with a smile, "we had an instant connection, and here we are today."

The memory got to me. I could feel my eyes water.

Sarah clapped. "Not a bad job telling the story, Mike. Not as good as Dawn, but pretty close."

"My boy, a hero," Vic said. "Nicely done, Mike. Now, about us shooting that gun tonight."

Sarah rolled her eyes a final time and regarded me with concern. I tried to avoid her gaze, but she continued to stare at me as the men talked.

"You haven't been yourself since I got here," she said. "What's wrong?"

"Nothing," I lied. I raised my head and met her stare. I couldn't lie anymore. I needed to do something. "I just... can't pretend anymore about any of it. I can't pretend that I don't know what's happening."

"What's going on?" she said. She glared at Vic. "Did you tell her?"

"What, about your work? No!" Vic said with a laugh. "I thought you were going to wait to tell everybody."

"What are you guys talking about?" Mike asked.

"She's quitting," Vic said abruptly. Sarah shook her head.

I looked at Sarah, my mouth wide. "You're quitting?

"Yes," Sarah said. "It's just too much. I can't handle Ronald. I can't handle the customers. I can't take it anymore. It's too much. I thought maybe that's why you were upset. I thought, you knew... I told Ron not to tell anybody. I just wanted to quietly leave. I knew I was going to see you this weekend and I was going to tell you. I didn't want it to ruin everything planned with Mike, but I just can't take it there anymore."

"That piece of shit Ron," Vic said with a sneer. "I'd like to show him that gun."

Sarah hit him on the shoulder again. "Victor!"

"It's true. You told me how much you hate him."

Sarah shook her head. "It's mostly the customers. I can't handle all these negative calls and confrontations all the time. It's just too much." She looked up at me. "I don't know how you do it. You're just able to take all that negativity, all those terrible abusive comments, and... smile."

"I didn't know you were going to quit," I said quietly.

"Then what is it? Why do you look like the world's about to end?"

I gazed out the front window, hoping to find an answer. Hoping to see her. Hoping to make sense of everything that was happening. I'd tried pretending that everything was normal, but it wasn't.

Amber Townsin was out there in the woods, and I was stuck here with these people, pretending that everything was okay, pretending that I didn't know what was going on. But I did. I knew exactly what was going on. And I couldn't take it anymore.

"I have to go," I said, standing up abruptly. "You have to go too."

"Where are you going? You're freaking me out to be honest."

"You should be!" I barked.

Victor, confused, stared outside at the snow. "Don't worry. We knew there was going to be a blizzard. We figured we'd be shacking up with you guys this weekend anyways. It's okay if the roads aren't ready on Monday. Please, give me a reason not to go to work." He chuckled, then turned to Sarah and said, "You don't even have a job, so we have nothing to worry about."

Sarah put up her hand. "Don't worry, guys, it's okay. If you really want us to leave, we could try. But in this blizzard if we get stuck out there in the middle of nowhere..."

"Is this our first couples' fight?" Vic said with a smirk. "Look, we can go if we're not welcomed here, or whatever is happening right now, but outside is the last place I would want to be."

Amber only had on a sweatshirt and socks. No shoes. She was in danger. And every minute I sat at this table pretending otherwise, all I was doing was contributing to her murder, if she wasn't already dead.

Mike stared at me. "Hun, it's okay. Sit down. These are our friends."

I shook my head. "What did you do?" I said, staring at my husband. Mike's smile vanished from his face. Vic and Sarah exchanged a glance. I slammed my hand on the table. "Why did you have her?"

"What are you talking about?" Mike raised his hands in the air, surrendering.

"Amber Townsin. Why did you have her in our basement?"

Victor leaned towards him. "Who's Amber and why haven't you told me about her?" He laughed. No one else did.

Sarah looked at me and then at Mike. "Is this an act? I don't understand."

"I've been acting all night!" I shouted. "Now I need answers, and help."

"Mike, what is she talking about?" Sarah asked again.

"Dawn... what are you saying?" Mike asked.

"The woman that you had in chains in the basement!" I shouted. "Her name is Amber Townsin. Why was she there? What were you planning on doing to her?"

Mike stood up from the table. "You're saying there's a woman chained in our basement?"

I nodded intensely. "You had her eating dog food and drinking from a bowl, shitting in a bucket. Why was she there? Who else have you done this to?"

Mike didn't answer and continued to gaze blankly around the room.

"Now she's gone," I said. I pointed my finger at my husband. "You had your cell on you when we were in town! Who did you call when we left? Who went into the butcher room and took Amber? Where is she now?"

Vic let out a breath. "Okay, I'm confused. So, there's no woman in the basement?"

I looked at Sarah. "You need to grab your phone and call 911."

"What is she talking about?" Vic said, standing up as well. "The butcher room? You had a girl in the butcher room?... I told you not to keep her there." Mike stared at Vic. I turned my head to him too, and he smirked back at me. "I told you to move her." Vic pointed a finger at Mike as intensely as I had. "I told you not to keep her in the cabin to begin with. I told you we were coming for your surprise party. Did you forget old man?" Mike gazed at him, and me, confused.

Vic turned to me. "How much do you know?" he yelled.

Sarah tugged on his sleeve. "What the hell are you saying, Vic? Who is Amber?"

"Well, she's the girl that was in the basement. The one that Mike and I are going to kill."

CHAPTER 22

Amber

I sprinted through the moonlit forest, my lungs burning with every step, fueled by adrenaline and determination. At times I felt a similar sensation I had in track and field in high school.

I heard the man in the mask behind me, yelling, "Where are you going to go?"

As I continued to run, I would hear him less, but I knew he was still there. Chasing me, tracking me, searching for my footprints in the snow. Eventually, he would find me, I knew. He still had his rifle on him.

My track and field coach, Mr. Anderson, was a huge motivation for me in high school. He knew when I wasn't driven. He would yell at me to snap out of it and pick up my stride. Sometimes he would attempt to follow me, usually lagging behind, yelling at me, pushing me to go faster.

Coach Anderson was more upset than me when I stopped going. He felt I had it in me to get a scholarship with my athleticism.

Why had I given up? I couldn't remember now.

"I will find you!" my captor screamed into the night. I looked back. He was barely visible, but I saw him moving towards me.

I can't give up now, I know.

Without boots on, my feet were freezing. I had no jacket, toque, or even a pair of mittens. Everywhere I went, the snow left a trail for him to find me. When my fear became strong to the point that I wanted to give up, I would hear Coach Anderson yelling at me to keep going. It was as if he was out here in the snow with me, motivating me to stay alive.

When I was in the basement, my captor warned me that if I didn't follow his instructions, he'd shoot me. When he raised the gun and fired, it struck the cement wall. The pain in my ears was immense, and I covered my head.

I listened to what he told me after that. I put my hands on the wall, facing away from him. I heard him move the bucket and put the chair against the wall. He took out a key from his pocket and took off the chains and the handcuffs.

Then he pointed the gun at my head. I felt the muzzle against my hair.

"If you move, you're done, little doggie," he threatened.

I didn't test him. I knew he meant it. I stood there until he instructed me to move. I turned and that monstrous wolf's face snickered at me. I peered at the eyes beneath the mask, and I could see how enraged he was.

"Move it," he said, pushing me towards the door. "Up the stairs and go out the front door."

"I need shoes," I said before taking a step up the stairs.

He pointed the gun at me in response. "No more talking back. I've had enough of you. Do as I say, now! Or I'll blast you away right here."

I listened and reluctantly went up the steps until he shoved the barrel of the rifle against my back hard and I fell face forward into the stairs, bruising my forearm.

"Get up," he said. "Move, faster, up the stairs and out the door, right now."

I stood up, checking the bruise on my arm. I wanted to turn to him and tell him more of what I thought of him but knew better. When I got to the main floor, I walked across the room and opened the cabin door. My captor watched me, and went to a kitchen table, grabbing a beat-up backpack, tossing it over his shoulder. I looked outside at the snow falling. I nearly lost my balance when I stepped onto the porch. If it wasn't for me putting out my hand and stabilizing myself on a red mailbox beside the door, I would have fallen again.

"Where are we going?" I asked.

"My car," he said quickly. "Now, move it. That way." He pointed towards a grouping of trees. I did as I was told, my socks soaking quickly on the snow-covered ground.

He pointed in the direction of his car. “Keep moving, faster.”

“Please,” I pleaded. “If I had shoes I could.”

The man with the wolf's head shook his head no, and he pointed the rifle at me again. “You need to listen. Move it!”

I took another few steps and pretended to lose my balance, falling to the ground. I could hear him audibly sigh.

“I don't have time for this shit,” he said. “You need to stand up.”

I closed my eyes and cried without tears. I wasn’t crying because I wasn’t sad. I was angry.

“I can't get up,” I cried out. “I can't... I can’t do it.”

I waited until he bent over to help me. When he did, I made my move. I pushed my head upwards into the wolf mask. I could feel his face as I crashed into the mask with the top of my head. I shoved him until the gun fell behind him. He threw a punch at me, and I ducked, digging my fingers into his neck. I took a chunk of skin in my nails. He screamed in pain and tossed me to the ground with ease. He turned and grabbed the gun quickly, and as he did, I ran as fast as I could into the forest.

As I continued to run, I could hear him chasing me. My body was sore, my legs felt wobbly, my feet were cold, but my heart would not give up.

"Keep going, Amber!" Mr. Anderson's voice yelled at me. "Don't give up like you did on me! Don't give up again!"

I continued to run, with him shouting in the background, until I finally saw in the dark a yellow Jeep parked on a trail. I ran up to it, but no one was inside. I peered into the driver's side window, hoping to find keys, but there was nothing but a hunting magazine.

And that's when I saw it. In the backseat was a wolf mask, just like the one the man had on right now. There25 were two masks.

Who was the other one for?

"You're not going to get away," my captor yelled, getting closer, and I screamed as loud as I could, running back into the dark woods.

I hid behind a tree, and peered around it. In the distance, I could see the flannel jacket of my captor. He was no longer wearing the wolf mask but was too far away to see his face. The moonlight exposed the rifle still in his hand. He lowered his head and studied the snow. And at that moment, I knew he was tracking my footsteps. I didn't have much longer before he would find me. He had proper clothes on, boots and a gun. All I had were my socks and my determination to survive.

I ran into the woods, trying to put as much space as I could between me and him, when I stopped in my tracks. A cabin.

Several cars were parked outside. I ran closer

until I noticed the red mailbox beside the front door.

It was the same cabin that I escaped from. Somehow, I had managed to go in a complete circle in the dead of night.

I heard a blast behind me, and I felt a whizz by my head. I didn't turn back. My captor was most certainly there, attempting to aim better. What I did see was a red dot that moved across the snow until it vanished.

I ducked and ran, zigzagging until I made it to the cabin. I ran up the steps as quickly as I could and opened the door.

CHAPTER 23

Dawn

The tension in the room was palpable as Mike's voice echoed through the cabin, his confusion and anger directed at Victor. "What the hell are you talking about?" he yelled.

Victor responded with a chuckle, his laughter only growing as he saw my face. "Your wife isn’t the only one who acts well," he said, his words adding to the unease in the room.

But all I could focus on was the expression on Mike's face. It was genuine, sincere, and showed that he had no idea what was happening. He looked just as scared as I felt.

"You didn't know about her, did you?" I said, directing my question to Mike.

He stared at me in disbelief, his expression one of utter bafflement. Sarah too, seemed lost in the conversation, her voice trembling as she spoke. "What are you saying? I don't understand. You guys are scaring me. Can you all just stop?" She looked at Victor with a plea in her eyes.

Victor, understanding the gravity of the situation, stopped laughing and said, "Sorry," in a quiet voice.

Mike scanned the room, still trying to make sense of things. "Are you saying there's a woman downstairs in the basement?"

I nodded; my voice filled with urgency. "She was in the basement. When we came back from grocery shopping, she was gone. Her name is Amber Townsin, and I think she's in great danger. We have to call the cops."

The confusion was evident on everyone's face, Victor no longer found the situation amusing, and Mike couldn't fathom what was happening.

"Amber Townsin," Sarah repeated, her voice barely above a whisper. She gazed questioningly at Victor. "I heard that name on the radio driving here. She's the missing university student, right?" Victor lowered his eyes.

Mike stared at me. His voice filled with hurt. "Why didn't you tell me? Why didn't you tell me about her when you first saw her?"

I couldn't bring myself to meet his gaze, instead, I glanced at the fridge in the kitchen. "We need to call 911," I said, avoiding his question.

Suddenly, a loud blast interrupted our conversation.

"That's a rifle shot," Mike said, his voice filled with alarm. Soon after, a woman's scream filled the air. My heart dropped as I knew it was Amber.

Without hesitation, Victor ran to the couch and grabbed the gun. "It's not loaded!" Mike yelled, but Victor ignored him, holding the rifle firmly.

I made a move to open the door, but before I could, it was flung open and slammed into my face. Amber Townsin stood in the doorway, her eyes wide with fear as she took in the faces staring back at her. Her gaze met mine and I could see recognition in her.

"Hide!" she screamed. She saw the blood streaming down my face from where the door had struck me, and she pulled me to safety behind it.

Victor, gun in hand, aimed it towards the doorway as Rick entered the cabin, his own rifle aimed at us. Rick fired three shots at Victor, one of them striking him in the neck. He fell to the floor immediately, coughing out a scream.

Sarah's shriek filled the air. Rick then turned towards her, the red dot of his rifle's sight moving until it was aimed at her forehead. The sound of the shot was deafening as Sarah slumped into the chair, her face falling into the plate of food on the table.

I let out a scream as Amber covered my mouth, trying to silence me.

Rick turned his attention towards us, his rifle aimed at my head. "I'm sorry, sister," he said, his voice filled with a mixture of regret and determination.

CHAPTER 24

Vic rolled around on the floor, covering his throat, blood gushing from his mouth. Sarah lay motionless at the table. Rick aimed his gun at me, but I stood my ground, shielding Amber behind me.

Mike screamed and tackled Rick from the side.

"Run!" Amber screamed at me.

She grabbed me by the shirt and pulled at me until I ran with her outside into the falling snow. I could still hear Rick and his brother wrestling on the ground, yelling at each other. The shouts from inside the cabin grew louder.

As we ran into the cold winter night, I realized that neither of us were prepared for the freezing temperatures, as we'd left without boots or jackets.

"There's no time to stop!" Amber yelled as she held my hand, and we ran deeper into the forest. I reluctantly followed her, checking back every so often at the cabin.

Suddenly, a gunshot rang out, and I froze, my thoughts turning to Mike, my husband, whom I had abandoned to his fate. I stopped. Amber tugged on my arm, but I shrugged her away.

"Mike!" I yelled.

"Stop!" Amber shouted. "He's going to find us."

I turned to Amber. "I left him. I left him to be killed. All because I didn't trust him."

Amber tugged on my hand again and said, "We have to go if we want to survive this. Now, let's move."

As we ran, two more shots came from inside the cabin. I turned and screamed my husband's name again. "Mike!"

Amber pulled me towards some thick bushes. "Don't make me leave you, Dawn. We have to go – now! Please!"

After a few moments, I could hear my name being shouted. "Dawn! Dawn! Stop!" It wasn't Mike, but Rick. "You don't understand!"

I looked at Amber. "Okay, let's move," I agreed. We hurried into the forest as fast as we could manage.

It was a daunting task. The snow was coming down heavily, making it difficult to see where we were going. The cold was biting at our skin, numbing our fingers and toes. I could feel the chill creeping into my bones. My feet were already numb, and each step was a struggle as I fought to keep them from freezing. Amber was struggling as well, her teeth chattering as she ran beside me. We weren't going to make it much further.

We trudged on, each step becoming harder and harder. I could feel the fatigue setting in, and my mind was beginning to wander. I thought about Mike. I thought of the three shots from the cabin. I thought of Sarah and Victor, dead, now joined by my husband.

Then I thought about Junior.

The thought of my son snapped me out of my daze. I pulled back on Amber's hand, forcing her to stop. "We need to come up with a plan. Rick knows these woods better than us. He will find us."

"When I was running before he tracked my footsteps."

I peered up at the heavy snow coming down. "Thankfully, Mother Nature might help us with that, and cover up our tracks." I pointed in the distance. "Crescent Lake is that way." I pointed up a hill. "Over there is the highway."

"Let's go!" Amber called, trying to take me towards the highway.

I held her hand and shook my head. "That's exactly where Rick will hunt for us. Rick knows exactly where the highway is."

"So what do we do?"

Even at night in the snowfall, I knew the walking trail we were on, and where it led to. I turned to Amber. "I have a plan."

CHAPTER 25

We made our way up the trail to Harold Vaughn's' cabin. Our feet ached with the cold and my fingers were numb, the only way to warm them being tucking them under my armpit. As we trudged through the snow, the wind howling around us, I couldn't help but reflect on how different this hike was from the ones I had taken with Mike in the past. We had always been well prepared, with warm jackets and sturdy hiking boots, but now, Amber and I were ill equipped for the harsh conditions of the forest.

Finally, the cabin came into view. I'd seen it before, occasionally spotting Harold sitting on the porch, absorbed in his woodcarving. The cabin was small and rustic, made of rough-hewn logs that looked as if they had been cut from the surrounding forest. A chimney jutted out from the roof, sending plumes of smoke into the air. But now, the lights were off, and I couldn't help but feel a sense of unease.

I feared the worst, that he wasn't home. It couldn't have been too late; I prayed he had gone to sleep. Harold Vaughn was the only hope that Amber and I had to get out of this alive.

"Hurry," I said, frantically. We ran to the door. Amber beat me to it. She peered through the windows into the darkness inside, then knocked on the door furiously.

"Mr. Vaughn!" I called out. "Please, hurry. It's me, Dawn. Dawn Nelson! Harold!" I yelled. "Please!"

A run-down truck was parked next to the cabin, and I knew Harold must be there.

“He has to be home,” I said. I knocked and yelled his name louder.

Amber glanced back into he woods behind us. "We can't be too loud... How old is this man?"

"Nearly seventy years old," I said, knocking again. "Harold, please open the door. Please wake up."

Amber put her hands over her forehead and peered inside again. "I still don't see anything. Maybe we should keep running?"

I knocked on the door again, this time lighter, almost giving up. Running through the forest without proper clothing and shoes seemed futile, a doomed effort that would lead to us being caught or succumbing to the cold.

"A light!" Amber said, pointing, and I saw a flicker in the window. "He's awake, I think. He's awake, thank God." She was barely able to contain herself.

I knocked again. "Harold, it's me. It's Dawn.

Please hurry."

The front door creaked open, and Harold popped his head out. "Dawn? What are you doing? What time is it?"

I pressed on the door in my urgency and opened it a little bit wider. He seemed taken back by that.

"Harold, please," I said. "We need to come inside. We're in trouble. He's trying to kill us. Mike's dead. Some of my friends were shot and killed."

Harold's eyes widened. "What? Mike's dead?"

"Rick killed him. He tried to kill me." With shaking hands, I reached for Amber, who was huddled next to me. "Rick had kidnapped her. It's why everything happened tonight. I found her in the cabin's basement, where Rick was keeping her. Now he's chasing us in the woods, and he has his gun... We need to call 911."

"Rick," Harold repeated. "Okay, calm down." He gestured for us to come inside. We dashed into his cabin, and he closed the door, checking around the forest as he did. He immediately ran to the back of the room and turned off the light.

"We have to be quiet," he said. "Good chance he heard you girls and could know exactly where you are. Where else would you go?" He put a finger to his mouth, and then went to the windows, closing the drapes.

"It's snowing heavily outside," I said. "We're hoping our tracks were covered as we ran."

“If you’re lucky, maybe,” Vaughn said. “But given our situation, I think not.”

Amber nodded at Harold, but I watched him intently. It was almost off-putting how quickly he understood what was happening. He didn’t seem scared by our presence, or worried about himself. He appeared to be problem solving on what to do next.

“We need you to call the cops," Amber said.

Harold shook his head. "I don't have a phone. I haven't had one in years."

Amber was surprised. "Who doesn't have a phone?"

"Got no one to call.” He chuckled. There are some blankets over there.” He gestured towards a pile of blankets stacked on a couch nearby. My eyes followed the direction he was pointing and were met with the unsettling sight of multiple taxidermized heads of animals mounted on the wall. It was a display not uncommon for someone like Harold Vaughn, a man of the wild. He noted our unease. "I understand. There isn't a moment to waste."

I pointed at the front window. "We need to get in your truck, and we need to leave before Rick finds us."

"We do need to run, that's right. But before we leave, you guys need appropriate clothes. In the bedroom, in the back of the closet, are my wife's clothes. Find something warm…” He turned and walked towards a staircase leading to the basement. "I'll be right back."

"Where are you going?" Amber asked.

Harold hurried as fast as he could. "To get my gun."

CHAPTER 26

With a sense of urgency, we quickly made our way to the cabin's only bedroom. I ventured to the closet, rifling through it until I found Harold's wife's clothing. Much of it seemed dated, as if it belonged to an older woman.

I picked up a sweater adorned with fluffy white balls, and Amber couldn't help but smirk. "Maybe this isn't your style," she said, trying to lighten the mood despite our dire circumstances. I smiled back, appreciating the moment of levity amidst the danger.

Amber found a black crew-neck sweater, which was a little tight on her, but it would serve as a temporary solution. I couldn't help but notice a picture frame on the nightstand with Harold and his wife posing in front of a beautiful lake. I noticed the scenery instantly. I had nearly died there myself the day I met my husband. It was Crescent Lake.

I stopped as I realized Anna Vaughn had actually died in the lake.

Mike had told me what happened to her. It was a boating accident, and she had drowned.

Harold had found her body.

I imagined Harold walking into the cold lake water, collecting the body of his wife floating at the surface, holding her tightly. My imagination was wild, but I knew I could have a similar experience soon and wouldn’t have to pretend to know what it would be like. Eventually, after the police found out everything, I would come back to the family cabin. I would come back with the police. I’d have to show them where my cabin was. Show them where my husband's body lay.

There was more than my husband. I thought of the last moments I saw Victor and Sarah alive. The expressions of fear they had before Rick murdered them. He would have killed me and Amber had it not been for Mike saving us.

Mike was the only reason I was still alive. Mike was also the reason I didn't say a word until it was too late.

I didn't trust my husband. I thought he was the one behind everything. I thought he was behind everything.

How could I ever think that the man I loved had done that? He couldn't hurt a fly. I’d taken his sadness the last past months to mean that something was terribly wrong with him. And when I came across Amber, bound and captive in the basement, the truth hit me like a ton of bricks. Mike wasn't just struggling emotionally, he was capable of murder.

If I could go back in time, I would have immediately spoken up and taken action. We could have safely rescued Amber together and brought her to the authorities. Instead, Mike was gone, and we found ourselves in a desperate situation, holed up in Harold Vaughn's cabin as we planned our escape.

Amber put a hand on my shoulder. "I'm sorry for your husband. His name was Mike, right?" I lowered my head. “I'm sorry, Dawn,” she repeated. She took a deep breath. “I’m sorry too for what I said before.”

“What did you say?” I was confused.

“I told you I would have left you if you didn’t come with me. Of course you wanted to go back and help your husband. I just need you to know, I wouldn't have left you. I don’t know why I said it.”

“We all say weird things when we’re scared,” I said. I’d acted the whole day as if everything was normal, even though it was the worse day of my life. To many that would have seemed much odder.

“I’m sorry for everything,” Amber said.

“Me too.”

“The man we ran from, the one who did this... he’s...”

"His name is Rick Nelson. He's my husband's brother.” In retrospect I should have known it was Rick from the beginning. How many red flags had he presented with over the years that he was capable of committing these heinous acts?

I shook my head. "We can discuss everything further once we're safely in town. Harold has a closet near the front door where we can grab some shoes."

We made our way to the living room, grabbing warm jackets for the journey ahead. Amber found a pair of boots that were too big for her but would have to do. Unfortunately, there wasn't a second pair of boots to be found, so I slipped on a pair of white sneakers.

Harold entered the room, rifle in hand and binoculars hanging around his neck. He asked, "Are we ready to head out?" Amber and I both nodded in agreement.

“Before we leave,” Amber said, "I really need to go to the bathroom."

He cocked his head towards the hallway. “It’s the first door on the right.” Amber hurried off.

Harold went to the front window and peered outside. "We don't have much time," he said. He lifted the binoculars and put them to his eyes, staring into the dark forest, watching for any movement. “When she comes back, when I tell you guys it's safe, I want you and Amber to run to the passenger side and get in. I’ll cover you from the window. I'm going to keep looking until I feel comfortable that there is no one out there looking back.” He reached into his pocket and gave me a set of keys. For a moment he paused and regarded me intensely. “No matter what happens, Dawn, you get to that driver's seat, unlock the doors for everyone. If you hear shots, wait for Amber to get into the truck before you take off. I'll stay behind and fight off Rick until you're safe."

"You need to come too," I said, panicking. "You can't stay here."

Harold shook his head. "I'll be just fine." He smiled. His teeth were still yellow and his grimace still ugly, but it now comforted me. "Besides, there's something I need to settle with Rick."

"What do you mean?" I asked, confused.

"I knew something was off with that boy. My wife knew it too. She knew before me. I should have listened better." He sighed and turned back to the window. "She had told me that Rick and Mike were an odd duo. Mike was level-headed, and Rick just seemed crazy. She said there was something about Rick that scared her, but she didn't know what it was. And she couldn't describe to me why she felt that way. I shrugged it off. I had known the Nelson family most of my life growing up here." He paused. "After... the accident happened with Anna, it was Rick who found her body and came and told me. I followed him back to Crescent Lake. I didn't want to believe what he had told me until I found her body. He had dragged her to the shore. I broke down, but still managed to thank Rick. At one point I glanced back at him. I guess he didn't expect me to see. He had this... expression that bothered me. He even smiled, until he saw me looking at him. I don't know why but that smile stuck with me for a long time. Ever since then, I thought something was wrong. I couldn't fight this- feeling I had that somehow, Rick wasn't telling me everything. Who could hurt my Anna though? She was a saint to the Nelson's growing up. Now, I know Rick is just crazy. It all adds up."

"Did the police say whether there was anything suspicious with your wife's drowning?"

Harold nodded. "At first they questioned Rick, and me. But eventually they said that… It was an accident. I accepted that but could never come to terms with it. Somehow, I always knew there was more. When you knocked on my door tonight, I knew… Rick is going to pay for what he's done, to all of us."

Amber came out from the bathroom and joined us.

"Today," he continued, "when I was hiking, I thought I heard a woman scream. And I thought it was coming from your cabin. And then I saw you, Dawn. I figured I must have just been hearing something you had on the television, or something." He turned back to the window. "None of that matters now. Next time I'll listen to my gut when I know something is wrong. The police are going to sort this out. They'll find Rick. You're going to get out of this. You too, young girl."

"Thank you, Harold," I said. I looked at Amber, who seemed pale, even with the warm clothes. “One last thing, is there anything that she can eat? Something quick, like a granola bar or something for the road. She hasn’t eaten all day.”

Harold gave me the binoculars. "Keep checking outside," he said. "Watch for any type of movement, any trees and bushes that are moving that don't seem to go with the wind. I'll be right back.” He gestured for Amber to follow him but quickly turned to me. “When you're looking out the window, don't stick your head out too far. You never know who's watching you.”

CHAPTER 27

Amber

I followed the old man named Harold into his kitchen, the tension building in my chest as he opened the pantry door and grabbed a bag. He quickly and efficiently loaded it with cupcakes, granola bars, and other food items.

The smell of neglect hit me like a wall. Dirty dishes were piled high in the sink and on the counter, crumbs and spills covered the table and the floor was sticky with who knows what. On the counter a stained coffee mug had a cartoon hand with a middle finger.

Harold added a box of crackers and a bag of chips to the bag before handing it to me. I thanked him, and that's when I saw a half-used bag of dog food. I found it odd that I hadn't heard of a pet of any kind since we'd been there.

"Do you have a dog?" I asked.

"I did. Jessie was a good old lab. A good pup. I had to put her down last year."

I cringed when he said he had to put her

down. The man with the wolf mask, Rick as I knew him to be, wanted to do the same with me only a few hours ago.

Harold then asked, "Your name is Amber Townsin, isn't it?"

"It is."

He smiled. "I heard something on the news. Your name has been broadcasted all around the county. It's a good thing you guys knocked on my door tonight. We're going to get you home."

"Thank you."

"And, speaking of that, it's time for us to leave." His smile vanished.

We went back into the living room and Dawn raised a finger in the air as she peered out the window.

"I saw something. I mean... I think I did. I don't know. It could have just been the wind."

Harold quickly walked up to her, took the binoculars, and began looking outside. "Okay. There's more guns downstairs. If I tell you to, I want you girls to go downstairs. Arm yourselves and wait. Wait in the basement."

When he said the word basement, my insides turned. I felt nauseated. A basement was the last place I wanted to be.

Harold nodded as he continued to search around the bushes where Dawn had pointed. "I don't know. I don't think I see anything."

I took a few steps backwards into the living

room, my heart fluttering in my chest. My heart jumped and I could feel my pulse quicken. My breathing was becoming labored. The dog food in the pantry and him telling me to go to the basement. It was all too much.

I thought about the yellow Jeep and the second wolf mask on the backseat.

There was more than one of them. One was Rick's. Who was the other mask meant for? I took another few steps backwards, staring at Harold and the rifle strapped to his shoulder. I turned and I stared at the wall of animal heads. They all seem to be mocking me with their dead eyes.

I took a deep breath, attempting to calm myself, but that was when I saw it. The last head in the collection. It was a wolf, its tongue sticking out at me. I screamed.

CHAPTER 28

Dawn

"Stop!" Harold demanded. "Stop screaming." He turned to me. "Get her to stop. Every living thing for five kilometers can hear that!"

I put my hands up to Amber and caressed her shoulders, trying to calm her. "Amber, you need to stop," I said calmly.

But Amber continued to wail, screaming as if someone was attacking her. I covered her mouth with my hand, but she shoved me hard against the wall. She continued to scream as she ran into the bedroom and closed the door.

Harold looked outside the window, his eyes wide. "You need to get her out of there. Tell her we're leaving right now. We don't have time for this." He looked at me, his face frightened.

He turned back and stood in the center of the window as he looked outside with his binoculars. A muffled blast came from outside. The window smashed, glass flying everywhere. I covered my face as shards came towards me.

Harold fell to the ground, his rifle falling beside him.

I quickly lay beside Harold and turned him over. His left eye was missing, a red hole with blood streaming out in its place. I screamed, louder than Amber. His body twitched on the floor.

"Harold!' I shouted. His body became altogether motionless.

I took the rifle and peeked through the window. I quickly fired towards the bushes where I saw the movement.

"Leave us alone!" I screamed. "Leave us alone!" I fired again.

The sound of the bullet rang into the dark night, echoing around the scenery. The trees continued to move in the wind as they naturally had but I could see nothing.

I heard a creak from the wooden porch. I held the gun tightly and turned, covering my face with my fingers, trying to get a grip. I needed to see outside. I needed to shoot him, but after what had happened with Harold I was scared to get up again.

The door creaked open and the footsteps came closer to me. I couldn't find the energy to fire. All I could do was cover my eyes. I couldn't see Rick. I couldn't handle seeing him with the gun in his hand pointed at me again. I couldn't watch as he ended my life.

I knew if I opened my eyes he would stare back at me, that smirk entrenched on his face.

When I didn’t hear any more footsteps, I slowly opened my eyes.

What I saw was much worse.

Mike had a rifle in his hand. He bent down and grabbed Harold's rifle and slung it over his shoulder.

"Mike," I said desperately. “I thought—”

Mike took out his cell phone from his winter jacket. He put it to his ear.

"I have them," he said.

CHAPTER 29

Amber

I locked the bedroom door and sat beside the bed, my body trembling and shaking. I could barely comprehend anything. All I could do was cry uncontrollably. Soon after, I heard gunfire, and after that a second shot, followed by Dawn screaming.

I managed to stop crying when I heard footsteps in the hallway, getting closer to the door. The sound stopped. I breathed in deep, wanting to scream, but unable to muster a sound.

The sound of a gentle knock surprised me. "Open the door," the man's voice said.

I knew instantly it wasn't Rick.

"No!" I screamed.

"It's Mike Nelson, Dawn's husband."

My eyes widened. We were certain that Mike had been killed by his own brother. I stood up and took a step towards the door.

"Where's Dawn?" I asked.

"Just open the door," Mike said. "We need to

talk."

Dawn yelled, "Don't open the door. Run! Run Amber!"

I hopped over the bed to a window, attempting to open it. The frosted pane was difficult to move.

A sudden, loud thud on the door jolted me into action. A wave of disappointment washed over me as I realized I had forgotten to undo the latch. In a rush, I frantically undid it and pushed.

Just as I had managed to open the window, Mike violently kicked down the door, sending it crashing to the ground with a loud bang. He strode into the room, his eyes quickly falling upon me.

He grabbed me and threw me to the bed, taking my hands easily behind my body.

"Just calm down," he said. "Relax. Stop fighting."

I screamed and yelled. I moved my body furiously, but he put his weight on top of me. He reached into his back pocket and grabbed handcuffs, and put them on with ease, connecting them behind my back. He pulled me up from the bed and grabbed my shoulder, dragging me from the bedroom as I screamed.

Dawn watched in horror, covering her mouth. “Let her go! Stop Mike!”

As we got closer to the front door, I heard a vehicle pull up. Mike opened the door, still dragging me. Rick parked his yellow Jeep and got out, making a face when he saw me and Dawn.

"Why didn't you kill them?" he said.

"Shut up," Mike told him. "Listen to what I say this time. Load them up."

"Where are we going?"

It was a question that had my attention.

Mike fixed the thick framed glasses on his face. "Back to my cabin."

CHAPTER 30

Dawn

The ride back I was silent and tense. Amber on the other hand continued to curse at Mike and Rick. Rick would occasionally glance behind him, threatening Amber's life if she didn't quiet down. Mike ignored her.

I sat quietly in the backseat. All I could do was stare at the back of my husband's head. Mike was obsessed with his ever-growing bald spot. One time he even asked me to measure it. I thought he was joking until he brought me the tape.

At night, when Junior was asleep and we would relax on the couch, talking and watching television, I enjoyed stroking his hair. He would lay back on me, taking up most of the couch, and I found comfort in comforting him, caressing his hair, making sure not to touch the bald spot and restart his hairline insecurities all over.

I loved it. I had missed spending time with him like that. Before we got to the cabin, he was ignoring me more and more. He was leaving the house. He said he wanted time to himself. Now I knew that was a lie.

He wanted to spend time with more girls like Amber Townsin, in the basement of our cabin. How stupid was I for not seeing him for what he was. Now I stared at his bald spot in Rick's Jeep, wishing I had something hard to strike his head with instead of caressing it.

It wasn't long until we were back at our family cabin. Rick parked behind Sarah's car and gestured for Amber and me to get out. He raised a gun at us, his voice cold and demanding as he told us to go back inside the cabin.

As we walked up the front steps and I opened the door, I couldn't bring myself to look at the scene inside. My eyes were closed, trying to block out the horrors that must be waiting for me. But eventually, I opened them, only to be met with the gruesome sight of Victor, lying on the floor with his hands clutched to his throat. His eyes were wide open, staring blankly at the ceiling above him, a bullet hole square in the middle of his forehead. Sarah sat at the dining table, her head slumped forward, the cheerful woman now a lifeless corpse.

"Back downstairs!" Rick demanded. I slowly walked past Victor, stepping over his body. Amber did the same, following me. Amber had stopped cursing at Mike and Rick at the sight of my friends' bodies.

I felt dizzy as I got closer to the stairs.

The sight of the murders, the tension between the brothers, the feeling of being trapped in the cabin, all of it was overwhelming.

"Keep moving, Dawn," Rick commanded. I gazed at my husband, waiting for him to say something, to stand up for me. Instead, he stared back at me coldly.

"Listen to Rick," Mike said, shifting the frame of his glasses on his nose.

I could see Amber was also in shock, her eyes wide with fear and her body trembling. I knew that she was feeling the same way I was, trapped and with no way out. We were both at the mercy of these two violent men, and the thought of what they might do next made my blood run cold.

I thought I knew who my husband was until I found Amber. She opened my eyes, and I wish I'd never seen what I had.

Mike was a monster.

Rick took a step towards me, and I quickly started to move to the stairs again, taking my time walking down to the basement. I knew where they wanted us to go, of course. As I entered the butcher room it was pitch black inside, and I quickly pulled on the string in the middle of the room, turning on the light.

Rick looked at Mike. "We just need to end this."

"I told you to shut up," Mike barked. "You ruined my life! You... killed my friends. You wanted to kill my wife, the mother of my child! Did you even think of Junior? I have a kid, Rick! What would Junior do without her?"

"You and I did fine without a mom," Rick said coldly. "Dawn saw everything. You and I both know this has to end. Stop making it worse for yourself..." He pointed a finger at Mike. "And just finish this!"

Mike swatted his brother's hand away, grabbed Rick by his shirt, and shoved him hard against the wall, pinning him.

"I told you to shut up, Rick!" Mike shouted. He breathed out deep, and let out a guttural scream, letting go. He turned his back and stared at me. "You messed up everything for me, Rick."

Rick moved his rifle from his shoulder and held it tightly, but didn't raise it. "You and I aren't going to go another round, brother. Don't put your hands on me again. It's time that you come to back to reality."

Mike shook his head. "You ruined my life," he repeated.

Rick regarded him with disgust. "I was trying to be a good brother! The girl – she was supposed to be your present." Mike made an equally disgusted face. "I had everything planned. This was supposed to be a weekend for us. Like how it used to be! I've seen how depressed you've been lately. I know you miss it. I know you wanted to do it again. When I was working late at the university and I saw this girl, I knew she'd be perfect for you. Perfect for us! You didn't tell me you would be at the cabin this weekend! That's on you! I even waited, freezing my ass of in the woods, hoping you would leave so I could get rid of the girl. If you told me you were having a party here tonight this-."

"I didn't know!" Mike shouted back. He glanced at me for a moment. "It was a surprise."

I looked at Amber, who stood in the corner of the butcher room, her head lowered. When I turned back, Mike was staring at me intensely.

He breathed out deeply and turned to Rick. "You're on cleanup duty."

"What?" Rick said.

"Cleanup duty!" Mike repeated loudly. "My friends, you take care of it. Clean up the cabin. Also, you're going to have to go to Harold Vaughn's house. Fix the window. Tape it up with plastic or garbage bags, or whatever. Clear out the body. There's a broken door in one of the bedrooms. Fix it."

"Tell me, dear brother, why the hell am I going to fix a broken door and window? The man's dead."

"Exactly," Mike said, matter-of-factly. "At some point, someone might come and ask questions. They'll see the broken window and a broken door, and of course Harold. But if they come and they see a broken window that's been fixed, and they don't notice a busted down door, with nobody inside, there's not going to be too many questions. Who's going to kill someone in their house and then fix it? When the weather clears, we'll get rid of Harold's truck, and Vic and Sarah's cars too.

Rick had a smirk on his face. "See, this is why I missed you, brother. I don't think of details like this. It's why I need you. We could do this together again."

Mike shoved him hard against the wall and pointed a finger into his brother's chest. "I told you: I'm done! I told you and Dad I'd never do it again. Now," he said, taking a step back, "there's a lot to clean up. Get started. Start with Vaughn's house."

Rick nodded. "I told you, though, don't touch me again."

Mike took a step closer to his brother. There were only a few inches between them. Rick was tall, but Mike slightly taller. My husband looked down at him intensely. My husband, the one who I assumed could never hurt a fly, frightened me even more at that moment. I was worried they would shoot at each other.

I glanced at Amber, who was moving closer to the door as the brothers faced off. I realized at that moment what Amber had seen. This could be an opportunity to escape.

"Don't test me," Mike whispered.

Rick raised a finger, and jabbed it into Mike's midsection. "Don't let them get away," he said. Rick moved his finger, and pointed it at Amber, while maintaining his stare at Mike. “Don’t you move any further, little doggy. Or I will put you down.” He smiled at Mike. “Stop being so tense, brother.” He flicked Mike’s nose with his finger, making a bloop sound, and laughed, before leaving the room and heading up the stairs.

Mike slowly turned his head to me, before leaving the butcher room.

“Mike,” I called out to him. “You can't do this! Please! I'm your wife.”

Mike cocked his head as if considering my request. He stepped outside the room and came back with a bucket. He put it on the floor, and left the room, closing the door behind him.

CHAPTER 31

This time, I was trapped with Amber in the basement. We were the only two survivors of brothers twisted killing spree. We were both quiet, understanding the gravity of our situation. Eventually, Amber sat down on the steel chair in the corner while I sat on the butcher table on the other side.

I thought of Mike. Rick had said that Amber was supposed to be his birthday present. He suggested that Amber wasn't the only woman they had done this to. How many times? How many women? What did he do to them after kidnapping them?

I knew the answer, of course. I've heard true crime stories, or news articles talking about missing women across the country. How many of them met their fate at the hands of a man like Rick – or my husband?

Rick said that Mike stopped, though. Why? My mind continued to race. What would the news article say about me and Amber when their plans were finished? What would Junior know? Would I disappear, like so many other women have? Would my son think I abandoned him? What kind of man would my little boy grow to be if raised by a murderer like Mike?

Mike mentioned his father. Albert Nelson was a hard man, I knew. Raising his sons as a single man would not have been easy. What did he teach them? Was everything that happened to Amber the result of Albert Nelson's parenting?

Mike said he'd told Rick and his father he was done. Done with what?

Kidnapping? Murder?

What type of family murders women together?

I thought of Junior again. How would Mike parent our son without me? Would he teach Junior the same things his father taught him? Would he and Rick bring my son to the family cabin someday and continue the tradition the Nelson family had, with another woman locked up in the butcher room?

I covered my head with my hands to try and calm my thoughts.

I could see Amber was busy as well. She was a young, beautiful woman who had a full life ahead of her. Without a miracle, her full life would take a shortcut to an unmarked grave. So would mine.

I couldn't help but stare at Amber's white sweater, emblazoned with the logo of the University of Calgary. In an attempt to take my mind off of our predicament, I asked her what she was studying.

Amber raised her head at me. Her eyes were intense, and full of rage. She took a deep breath.

“I'm in my first year of law.”

“Wow, you must be a real smart woman. I barely managed to graduate from my arts degree. What kind of law do you want to practice?”

Somehow asking her questions made me feel better. I was able to forget that I was trapped in my basement with her.

“It's only the first year,” she said. “But I wanted to do criminal law and be a crown attorney.”

I nodded. It was admirable. She wanted to put away the bad guys. Give them their deserved justice. It was also ironic, since it was the bad guys who might now be the end of her.

I felt short of breath thinking of that, and tried to come up with another question. I inhaled deeply. “Why would you want—”

“Can you just stop it?' she interrupted. “Can you stop asking me questions? Can you stop pretending your husband and his brother aren’t going to kill us? I’m not ever going back to school. I’m not going to finish.” She stared at the ceiling. “They’ll never give me the chance, like they will you.”

“What do you mean, like me?”

She scoffed. “Here I am, talking to the wife of

one of them... Why didn't you help me?"

"I tried," I said. "I tried to call the police... You have to understand, this doesn't make sense to me either. I had no clue."

"You had no clue that your husband was killing women? How blind could you be? How could you not know this was happening?"

"I didn't!" I shouted. "Mike was a good husband. He always treated me nicely. He never hit me. Never cursed at me, never raised his voice. We have a son. His name is Junior. He's six years old now... And Mike was a good father to him. Never hit him. Hated to discipline him. Until I found you in the basement, he was the perfect husband. He's not, I know."

"That's the only right thing you've said all day. He's not a good husband, or a good father... and you're the dumbest person I've ever met! If you'd got help for me, we wouldn't be trapped here! But that only matters for one of us, doesn't it? You were too busy looking out for yourself to get me help!"

"I'm trapped here too!" I shouted back.

Amber stood up from the chair and walked towards me. "You know I'm going to be the one that's killed, not you!"

"I'm down in the basement. Stuck here, just like you. I'm not upstairs with them."

"Ha! Do you actually think you and I are equal in this? I'm the one with the handcuffs on. That's because I'm the one that's in danger, not you."

I lowered my head. As much as I would love to believe what she said. It was hard to see anything more than the obvious conclusion that Rick had in mind for us both.

Amber shook her head and scoffed again. "You're going to get out of this, not me. I see how your husband looks at you. Do you think it's how he looks at me? To them, I'm just an animal. Something that Rick wants to... put down. You're Mike's wife. You don't think that changes everything?"

The sound of footsteps descending the stairs broke our tense conversation and sent a wave of dread crashing over me. I could feel my pulse quicken and my palms began to sweat.

The steps were steady and measured, not rushed or panicked. Whoever was coming down the stairs knew exactly where they were going and what they were doing. I couldn't shake the feeling that our captors were coming to finish us off.

Amber walked back across the room and sat on the steel chair, her eyes wide with fear. She seemed to sense my gaze and turned to me.

The footsteps reached the bottom of the stairs and began to approach the door to our prison. My heart was pounding in my chest so loud it felt like it was going to burst. I could feel my body tensing, preparing for the worst.

With a sudden clang, the door was thrown

open, and Mike stood in the doorway, his gun in his hand. He stared at us with cold, dead eyes, and I knew that our time was up.

His eyes softened as they fixed on me. "We need to talk."

CHAPTER 32

Amber looked back at Mike.

"She has to stay," he said firmly.

She pursed her lips, and glanced at me with a smirk before turning and facing the wall. I knew exactly what the facial gesture meant. I told you so, her face read.

"Come on, Dawn," Mike said in a calm voice. "Let's leave." He reached out his hand to me, but I didn't take it. Instead, I left the room on my own. Mike closed the door behind him and locked it with the deadbolt. "Let's go to our bedroom."

I glanced at the stairs going up. "It's okay," he said. "Rick's not here. He's at the neighbor's house. It's just you and me."

I walked up the stairs with Mike behind me, his rifle over his shoulder. Upstairs was still a mess. The bloodstained room still contained my friends' bodies. I let out a breath, my anxiety rising. My heart was beating faster, despite me trying to control my breathing.

Mike lowered his head. "I didn't mean for any of this to happen," he said. "If you want, you can close your eyes and I'll guide you through."

I ignored him, and walked into the room on my own. I stepped over Vic's body again and headed towards the main bedroom. I sat on the bed, and Mike entered the room, closing the door behind him.

Now it was him who took a deep breath. "I don't even know where to start," he said.

I let out a desperate laugh. "I just wanted us to have a fun weekend. I wanted you to have a good birthday. I wanted us to have... a fun time." I closed my eyes and thought of Sarah and Vic.

"None of this is your fault," Mike said. "None of it."

"Are you going to kill me?"

"No. Of course not."

“And... Rick?”

"I'm working on that." He nodded. "It's going to be okay."

I knew I had to ask, even though I was afraid of the answer. "What about Amber?" I said, my voice trembling. “What about her?”

Mike's expression was unreadable, but I could see the coldness in his eyes. "I don't think there's any way out of this for her," he said, his voice devoid of emotion. "I know that's hard to hear. But don't worry about Amber. I'm worried about... us."

My heart sank. I had been hoping for a different answer, something that would give me a glimmer of hope. But Mike's words were a death sentence for Amber.

In the basement, my husband told Rick he had stopped doing this to others. I had so many questions, and I was worried about the honest answers Mike would give me.

"How many women?" I asked. He didn't answer. "How many girls? How many? How many women have you killed? How long has this been happening?"

Mike took a deep breath and sat on the bed beside me. My instinct was to move further away from him. But the look in his eye... For a moment I felt he was the same man I knew before coming to the cabin this weekend. The man I knew before meeting Amber.

"My father," he said. "I'm not sure how many women he's killed. Rick too. I didn't know when I was a kid. I thought we had a happy family. I didn't realize, I didn't know. I didn't understand. It wasn't until I was an adult until I realized how much my father hated – *hated* – women. He made comments. He made jokes about them. Putting them down. He talked to Rick and me about the importance of men over the duties of women. Women... served man. That was their... purpose. I was young, and stupid." He let out a heavy breath. "And I believed it. Everything. We lived in his cabin. I didn't know any better. I looked back at what my father did. It was almost like he was training us as children to be like him. And eventually when we were older, he showed us how to do it. Showed us how to ensure men stay in power. How to remind *them* of their worth."

I watched my husband, my mouth gaping open. Even if I had the best acting skills on earth, I wouldn't have been able to hide my disgust. Mike knew instantly what I was thinking.

"I know. You have to understand how I was raised. How Rick and I were raised. My father was a very flawed man. After he showed us what to do with a woman, he showed us how to get away with it. I stopped, but Rick... who knows how long he's continued for. We don't talk about it... And now," he said to me, "you know everything. We thought we would never get caught. I thought I could keep this a secret. You need to know that I haven't done this in a long time. From the day I met you, I stopped. I promise on everything that means something to me in this world. I promise on Junior. I haven't killed or done anything terrible since the day I met you. You changed everything for me."

Mike reached for my hand, and I quickly moved it away. "I don't know what to say to all of this."

"I love you," Mike said, his voice softening. I glanced at him and saw his eyes start to water. "I never knew I could find someone who would... love me." He shook his head. "Who could actually love me. My father said love was bullshit. It was a fairy-tale women told themselves... I knew when I met you that day at Crescent Lake that he was wrong. He was wrong about... everything."

I lowered my head. Amber's words were starting to ring true. She knew the love my husband had for me. I was too scared to notice the difference in how I'd been treated compared to her since Harold's house.

"Smile," my inner coach told me. "Get into character!"

"I love you too, Mike," I said, reaching out for his hand. "All the years we've had together. When Junior was born, I loved you even more."

He grabbed my hand and held it tightly. "I know," he said softly.

"So, tell me what happens now."

Mike fixed his glasses on his face and took a deep breath. "We can make this work. We can make everything work for us. We can still have a good life together. A fun life together. A happy life together."

"And what about Junior?"

"He's going to be with us. We can stay in the cabin. All of us together."

"Hostage?" I asked. "What kind of life is that?"

"No!" he said, shaking his head. "We're going to have a good life here. All of us. You know we can't leave here after what you've seen. We can't go back to the life that we've had. We have to make a new one here. Our life can still be... perfect. We can still have that life together. I know it will be... hard at first, but we can make this work. Junior will be happy." Mike let go of my hand and stood up from the bed. "Junior won't have to know what it's like not having a mom."

CHAPTER 33

Soon after talking to me, Mike left the bedroom. As the door closed behind him, my heart was pounding in my chest. I did as I was told and didn't leave. I knew now wasn't the time to push my luck.

I lay there in the bed, staring up at the ceiling, trying to make sense of everything that had just happened. My mind was racing with the horror of what I had witnessed. The dead eyes of Sarah, the fear on Vic's face, it was all too much to take in.

I couldn't help but wonder what Mike was doing out there. Was he cleaning up the evidence of the murders? Disposing of the bodies? Was he making sure that there was no trace left of what had happened? The sound of something heavy dragging across the floor made my stomach turn. I tried to push the thoughts out of my head, but they were too overwhelming.

What would he do with them? With the bodies? I covered my ears and closed my eyes, wishing that this nightmare of a day had never happened.

As the minutes ticked by, the silence in the room was deafening. I thought about everything that Mike told me. It was his father who taught him to be this way. I couldn't help but think about all the other women who had met their end in this cabin.

A family of serial killers, and I inherited the cabin where they committed all their heinous crimes. The vacations that I'd had with Mike and Junior here were all overpowered by thoughts of dead women, and now of Vic and Sarah.

Mike said he'd stopped, but what about Rick? How many more women did Rick kill after we inherited the family cabin? How many times did Rick clean up after? How soon after Rick cleaned up did I bring my family to the cabin for a fun vacation? I cringed at the idea.

Rick hadn't returned from his 'clean-up' duties at Harold Vaughn's house. I thought about the old man. I wish I'd never knocked on his door. Had I not, he would still be alive. I'd brought him into this mess, and would have to live the rest of my life, no matter how short that might be now, knowing that.

Mike had confirmed that Amber was doomed to die as well. There's a very good chance I was still going to meet a similar fate.

Soon I heard Rick. He was never the quiet type. I could hear Mike talk in a low voice, unable to make out his words. Rick responded with shouting.

I knew what they were talking about.

I was supposed to be in the basement along with Amber. Now I'd been upgraded to the bedroom, locked inside. Still trapped, there was nothing I could do but wait. Stay with my thoughts of what my husband had done, of what Rick had done, of what their father had done. Think about how many young women had been murdered in this cabin. Think about Vic, Sarah and Harold.

I closed my eyes and tried to sleep. Thoughts of Amber made that difficult, those and what Rick was saying to Mike outside the bedroom door. It was obvious Rick was not happy with Mike's plans.

I couldn't disagree. It was a stupid idea after all.

Junior would come and live at the cabin with Mike and me? Where all the numerous women had been murdered? How long could that work for? What kind of a life would that be? Mike would never let me go out into the regular world again.

He'd said as much. He couldn't trust me. How could he trust me? He knew the first opportunity I had, I would try to escape, try and get help not only for myself but for Junior. He would never let me leave. He would never let Junior leave.

We would spend the rest of our lives trapped in this cabin.

After some time, a low knock on the door made me sit up at the front of the bed. Mike opened the door wearing a towel wrapped around his midsection. He sat on the bed beside me.

"I talked to Rick and he's okay with the plan," he said calmly. "Everything is going to be okay... You don't have to worry. Rick will listen to me. All I need from you is a promise: don't try and escape. Don't do anything... silly. Rick doesn't believe that this can work." Mike grabbed my hand. "But I know it can... We can still be a family." He stood up and grabbed some clothes from the closet.

"I've been thinking about your plan," I said. "What about Amber? Maybe... maybe she can stay with us. We don't have to..."

Mike interrupted me. "We'll talk about it later. Right now, we just need to focus on getting through this and making sure everything is cleaned up."

I nodded, feeling a sense of hopelessness wash over me. I knew there was no way out of this situation. I was trapped in a cabin with serial killers, and there was nothing I could do to change that. All I could do was wait and hope that somehow, things would work out in the end. All I needed was faith.

I turned away from my husband as he slipped under the covers. He wrapped his arms around me. Some married couples I knew slept in different rooms. Many enjoyed sleeping apart on opposite sides of the bed. Not Mike and I. Even when he was leaving the house at night, and me by myself, he would come home, get into bed, and... hold me.

"I love you," he whispered, nuzzling his head on my back.

I could feel a tear well in my eye. I wanted to burst out weeping. Instead, I took a deep breath, and attempted to compose myself. I needed faith to make it out of this alive. Faith, and some good acting skills.

"I love you too," I whispered back.

CHAPTER 34

At some point in the night, I opened my eyes. Mike was sleeping, snoring on his side. It was a sight I'd become accustomed to. He spoke in his sleep at times. One night he laughed, but not in his usual way. It was a high-pitched laugh, as if coming from a boy. It freaked me out that night, but eventually his sleep antics became comforting. It got to a point where his snoring was like white noise to sleep to.

Now, it caused me anxiety. It reminded me he was in bed with me. I didn't know if he would wrap his arm around me, or drag me out of the room, back to the basement with Amber.

Who was this man? Who was the person that I'd called my husband for the last thirteen years? Who was the man that I called father to my son? I wished none of this had happened. I almost wished I'd never found Amber Townsin. I could have gone on with the rest of my life not knowing.

Maybe Mike's plan wasn't so terrible after all. If we could get through everything that had happened and just... forgot about everything. I wished clearing my memory was as easy as deleting documents on a computer. I would quickly hover my mouse over Mike's psychopath folder and erase it.

I wish I could act my way through and pretend I still thought my husband was an angel. A man who wouldn't hurt a fly. I knew the truth now, though.

Suddenly, I thought of Amber in the basement. There were no windows down there. With her hands cuffed behind her back, she wouldn't be able to turn off the light. She would be forced to lay on the cement floor of a bright room, imagining her ultimate doom.

She might already be dead, even.

I knew Rick was back in the cabin. Mike had already confirmed that she wasn't going to live much longer. Mike hadn't left the room since coming from the shower. Who knew what Rick had been up to.

Mike let out a loud snore, his irregular breathing almost like he was choking in his sleep. Suddenly, the idea of sharing a bed with Mike made me want to vomit. I could feel my stomach turn in knots.

I slid out of bed as quickly as I could without waking him. His loud breathing stopped for a few moments before continuing. I let out a sigh of relief and opened the bedroom door quietly. I peeked outside and could see nothing but the darkness of the family cabin. The guest bedroom door was closed. I knew Rick was there.

"Don't do anything silly," Mike had told me.

Amber had told me something different. She told me that I was going to make it out of this, and now I knew for certain that she was doomed.

Mike's plan was for us to live together in the family cabin, happily ever after. A make-believe world where nothing wrong had happened here. It was a vision that I couldn't let Junior be a part of.

What if I just opened the door for Amber?

What if I just unlocked the dead bolt?

Rick would certainly want to kill me. But wasn't that my inevitable fate? Either it happened now, or ten years from now, when I became fed up with living trapped in the Nelson cabin.

I shut the bedroom door as softly as I could, but I didn't close it completely. I took small steps, careful not to make the old floor creak, which was nearly impossible. Every step came with a little noise, a squeak.

A voice inside told me to go back to the bedroom. Lay down beside your husband and pretend nothing was wrong.

But I couldn't do that. How much more pretending could I do? I took another step and the creak was louder. I stared at the guest bedroom door, waiting to hear movement. Waiting to see it swing open with Rick and his rifle ready to put me down.

Instead, it was quiet. I quickened my pace, understanding that the creaking was inevitable. I walked into the living room, glanced into the kitchen and stared at the table. The entire room was nearly spotless.

Even though her body had been removed from the dining table, it was hard not to think of Sarah. I stared at the floor where Vic used to be. The tiles were clean of any blood. The walls were white, with a hint of pine freshness. In the corner was a bucket, the water stained red, with a mop beside it. Cleaning supplies were on the table where Sarah's head used to be.

"And I bet you thought I wasn't good at cleaning." I turned around and Rick was on the couch. He sat up, rubbing the sleep from his eyes. "And... What are you doing?"

"I have to go to the bathroom," I said with a low voice. I could feel my body tremble at the sight of my brother-in-law. His rifle was leaning on the edge of the coach, near his feet. It was closer to me than him. He saw my gaze, and smiled at me, like he almost wished I would try and grab it to justify killing me to Mike.

"I'm sure you know where the bathroom is by now," Rick said, "and you passed it." He pointed down the hall. "So, what are you really doing?"

I avoided his death gaze. "I just had to see for myself. My friends were here, and now... it's like nothing happened."

"Isn't that the idea," he said with a sneer. "Nothing happened. That's Mike's grand plan, right?" He laughed. He gave me a sincere stare. "Is this the part where I'm supposed to say, I'm sorry, sister? I'm sorry I tried to kill you." He laughed again. I didn't respond. "That's fine," Rick continued. "I'll just say it, because Mike told me to. Sorry, sister. I tried to kill you. Now... are we better again? Can I be a part of the make-believe world that you and Mike and your son are going have? Sounds like a lovely place. Hummingbirds are always flying around, crime doesn't exist, and women make sandwiches all damn day." His smile vanished suddenly. "You know, if I had my way, this would go down differently, sister."

I saw his contempt and didn't respond.

Rick sneered at me. "Well, shit. I guess maybe there is a small chance this can work. You keep your mouth shut around me like this and maybe we can get along a hell of a lot better after all."

I took a few steps backwards, glancing at the rifle. Beside it was the beat-up beige backpack. A black patch with white lettering on it was sewn on the front latch, and read: "Bitches love me." He carried it everywhere with him, and the sight of the patch would always make me roll my eyes. Tonight I tried my best to leave without upsetting him.

"Goodnight," I said, turning back to the bathroom.

"Goodnight, sister," he said with a fake endearing tone. "Have good dreams." I took another step, when he called out to me. I turned and Rick stood up, grabbing his rifle and slinging it over his shoulder. "You guys may be good at pretending. You've always been the actress, Dawn, but you need to know. I looked up to my brother growing up. He was the oldest, and got the most praise from father. Dad gave him a lot of positive attention for what he used to do with your kind." He laughed. "Hell, I used to call him the Terminator. He's killed... many women. You look at me like I'm the bad man and yet you're going to go back to that bedroom and sleep besides one? It wasn't until he met you that things changed. He tried to be something he wasn't. I could see what that was doing to him. He needed to be... free again. You wanted to cage him, but you can't trap a beast. Eventually it breaks free. Mike's just a nicer-looking beast than me."

He paused, and examined my expression, which was hard to hide. What he said was disgusting, frightening. It made my insides roil thinking about it. The worst part was I knew Rick was telling the truth about my husband.

"Goodnight, brother," I said somberly. I saw a light from the stairs down to the basement. It was enough to give me hope that Amber was still alive.

I glanced back at Rick, and he grinned at me. "Goodnight, sister, " he said, swinging the rifle off his shoulder and tossing it on the couch. I walked towards the bedroom door. "Don't forget to take that piss now." He chuckled. "And get some good sleep. Tomorrow is going to be another long day. Tomorrow we're going to get rid of the loose ends."

CHAPTER 35

I woke up with the sun from the sheer curtains blinding me. I turned over but Mike was already out of bed. The door remained closed, but I could hear the brothers talking in the hallway.

Again, Mike spoke almost in a whisper, while Rick's voice boomed.

"Good!" Rick shouted.

I stood up from the bed when Mike came through the door. He stared at me with concern.

"Can I trust you?" he said, getting right to the point.

"You know you can trust me. How long have we been married, Mike?"

"Why did you leave the bedroom yesterday? Rick told me you left the room and he saw you."

"I had to go to the bathroom."

"You went past the bathroom and into the living room. Where were you going?"

"I wasn't trying to... escape," I said. "It's just new to me. Vic and Sarah. When I left the bedroom, I saw how clean the cabin was. It's weird. I wasn't trying to escape. I wasn't trying to do anything bad. I guess I just needed to see. It's weird not seeing them there. Their... bodies. It's as if nothing happened."

Mike sighed. "I wish nothing had happened. You know that. I never wanted any of this to happen. I just need to know that I can keep trusting you. It's really important... Why don't you throw on some comfortable clothes."

"Why?" I asked.

"You need to come out of the bedroom," Mike said. "I made you some breakfast. Sunny side up eggs the way you like them, with a side of bacon."

"Thanks," I said.

Mike stared at me a moment before leaving the room and walking down the hallway.

I took my time changing, and when I left the bedroom, Rick walked past me and opened the bathroom door.

He smirked. "Morning sister," he said as he shut the door behind him. He turned on the shower and I could hear him singing some operatic song to himself.

I walked into the living room and at the table where Sarah had been, there were two plates of food. Mike sat in his usual chair. At the other side of the table, where I'd sat last night, was a plate of food for me. I took my time sitting down. I used to love it when Mike made me breakfast. It was his favourite time to cook for our family.

I could never find the energy to wake up

as early as he did to make our grand breakfasts like him. I was the night owl in the relationship and would make fun of him when he would start passing out around nine while we watched television. He would make fun at me for being so groggy every morning.

Mike seemed to love mornings, and especially breakfast. At home, he would make a large breakfast for Junior and me. It would usually be pancakes drenched in butter, with maple syrup. There would always be a side of eggs. He scrambled his and Junior's but always made mine sunny side up, the way I preferred. For Junior, he made a smile out of the bacon on his plate.

"Sorry," he said, watching me. "No pancakes today. We didn't grab any batter at the grocery store."

"Next time, I guess," I said with a desperate grin. The way Mike watched me, I felt a sense of unease. It was almost as if every body movement I made was a test. I stared down at my plate and beneath my eggs that Mike had turned into eyes was a smile made out of bacon.

I nearly broke down in tears. I heard my acting coach say, "smile and the world will act differently. Smile and you will feel the difference inside you." I looked up at Mike, gave him a thin smile and nodded.

"Thank you," I repeated.

I picked up my fork and cut into my eggs. We

ate in silence. Mike took a sip of the orange juice.

He stood up and went to the refrigerator, grabbing my cell phone. He walked over to me and put it on the table and sat back down, staring at me.

"Call him," he said. "Talk to Junior. It'll make you feel better."

I wasn't sure if this was another test. What would he do if I scrambled to grab the phone? All I wanted in the world was to hear Junior's voice.

"It's okay?"

"We won't tell him about the cabin yet. When I pick him up at your mother's and bring him here, we can all talk together about it. Rick will watch you." I stared at him blankly. He nudged the phone on the table closer to me. "Just call him."

I reached for the phone, dialing my mother's number. I turned the phone and showed Mike that I was calling my mom.

He softened and nodded. "Thank you," he said in return. "That means a lot that you did that."

"Dawn?" my mother said when she answered.

I put the phone to my ear. "Hey, Mom."

"Dawn, honey, good morning. How was the night at the cabin? Did you and your friends have fun?"

I smiled, mustering all my facial muscles to not seem sad. "We had a great time. Everyone... had a great time. Board games all night." I looked up at Mike. "I just wanted to talk to Junior."

"And not me?" My mother laughed. "It's okay. I know how it is. At one point you were the center of my universe too, my love. Of course, let me get him. He's just watching a little bit of cartoons... but don't worry, he hasn't been doing that for too long."

"That's okay, Mom," I said with an authentic smile on my face. "I'm just happy he had a good night with you and Dad."

"We did have a great time. Okay, I'll go get him." She called out for Junior.

"Wait!" I shouted to her. Mike pursed his lips at me, waiting for what I would say next. I could feel his gaze, even though I tried not to notice.

"What is it?" my mom asked.

"... Nothing," I said. "I just wanted... to thank you again for watching him this weekend. It really means a lot to Mike and me... I... love you, Mom."

"Of course. Anytime you and Mike want to have a fun weekend, or date, we are always up to having Junior over. You guys can even do a nice getaway somewhere else besides the cabin. You should go to a beach resort or something. Get away from this cold! Just know that Grandma and Grandpa are always here."

"Thanks, Mom," I said, glancing at Mike.

"Here's Junior," she said.

"Mom?" I asked, but she hadn't heard me. It was probably better she didn't respond with Mike watching me. There was so much I wanted to say to her but Mike was listening and this was not a time to test his patience.

"Mommy," Junior said with his innocent voice. I immediately smiled and laughed in desperation.

"Junior, hi," I said, my eyes watering immediately. "How was the night at Grandma's?"

"It was good. We watched TV all night." In the background, I heard my mom shout that wasn't true.

I laughed. "Oh. What did you guys watch?"

"Grandma let me watch *Jurassic Park*."

"Oh boy," I said. "They watched Jurassic Park," I told Mike. He smiled back at me.

"Age appropriate," he said.

"That's what grandmas are for. Did you have a fun night?" I asked Junior.

"I did, Mom. Did you and Dad have fun with your friends too?"

"Yeah, we did, buddy. We had a great night."

"That's good, Mom. Is Dad there?"

I looked up at him. "He wants to talk to you, Mike."

"Tell him I'll call him after," Mike said. I stared at him for a moment and nodded.

"Dad's a little busy right now."

"I'm staying again at Grandma's house tonight, right?" Junior asked.

I nodded as if he was in the room. I quickly wiped the tears sliding down my cheek. "Yeah, of course."

"Good," he said. "We're going to watch another good movie tonight!"

"A PG movie!" my mother yelled in the background.

"That's okay, son. I want you to have a fun night with Grandma and Grandpa."

"Okay, Mom," he said. I couldn't get over how sweet his voice was. It was as if I hadn't heard my boy speak to me in forever. "Tell Dad I love him too, okay? You guys have fun, and I'll see you soon."

"Wait. I just want to tell you how much I love you, buddy. You're such a good boy." Tears streamed feely from my eyes. "You mean so much to me."

Mike stood up from the table and he stepped beside me. He reached out his hand.

"Is everything okay, Mom?" Junior asked. "You sound… sad."

"Everything's fine, buddy," I said. "... I love you."

"I love you too, Mom."

"Okay, buddy. I love you. I'll see you soon."

Junior laughed, his tone sweet and higher pitch. "You already told me you love me."

"Goodbye," I said. Mike put his hand under the phone trying to take it from me, but I clung on until I heard Junior's voice.

"Goodbye, Mom."

I let go of the phone and wiped the tears from my eyes. Mike slid it into his pocket and walked to the closet near the front door, opening it. He pulled out his jacket and boots.

"Let's go for a hike," he said calmly. He walked over to the kitchen counter and looked down at the collage of pictures that I'd made for him. He took the picture of his mother from the clip and stared at it. A red speck of blood from the massacre last night stained her image. "I want to visit my Mom again."

He put on his jacket, and swung the strap of his rifle over his shoulder.

"Why do you need to bring that?" I asked.

He shook his head at me. "You know I need to trust you more before we can walk around with no protection. This is to make sure. Let's go," he said, bending down to put on his boots. "There's more we need to talk about."

CHAPTER 36

The snowfall overnight had been relentless. What usually only took us minutes to walk now felt like an eternity. That could have been the cold feeling I got from Mike as we hiked, though. He was never talkative when we visited the spot where he remembered his mother. It felt different today. His lack of communication made me uneasy.

It was starting to snow again, light flakes flying from the sky. With the tall trees in the background and the sun shining down, it almost felt like we were walking through a Christmas globe. If it wasn't for Mike's tone before leaving the cabin, it would have been a beautiful hike with my husband.

Those times were done now.

Mike walked in front of me, quiet. He didn't even check back to make sure I was there. I understood that now wasn't the time to attempt an escape.

This was part of his test, and if I ran, that would be the end of me. He needed to trust me. He needed more proof for his brother that I wouldn't make waves.

Will that matter? I thought. Even if I went along completely with Mike's plan, Rick knew I couldn't be trusted. How much convincing would it take for Mike to agree to kill me?

Even if I wasn't murdered, how could I keep pretending to be a good wife to an ex-serial killer of women? It was a question that made my insides turn. Then I thought of Junior, living with me in my jail cell in the form of our cabin.

What would they do to him if he didn't go along with their plans?

I felt dizzy for a moment, and stopped trekking through the snow to catch myself, but failed. Nearly falling, I bent on one knee and caught my breath.

"Are you okay?" Mike asked. "Are you sick?" His light brown eyes fixated on me. For a moment, I wasn't scared. The empathy in his eyes confirmed how much he loved me. He was truly concerned.

"I'll be okay."

Mike walked back and extended his hand. I smiled at him before taking it. He lifted me up with ease, until I stood. He held on to my side to ensure I didn't fall.

He smiled back. Mike had a bad poker face. It was easy to tell when he was genuine or faking. The expression conveyed to me everything I needed to feel safe. Mike knew that his proposal for my new life would be hard to swallow. He likely assumed I would have some trouble coming to terms with it.

If I let him know how much disdain I had for it, he would likely kill me on the spot.

I grasped his hand tightly in mine. “Thanks,” I said. I glanced out into the forest before looking back at my husband. “I need you to know that I believe you when you say this can work,” I lied. “Talking to Junior this morning helped me see it.”

Mike pursed his lips and nodded. “Almost there,” he said, walking in front of me. I took a deep breath at his lack of response before reluctantly following.

We eventually made it to the familiar group of trees around the fallen one.

Mike walked up to the middle, the spot where he usually would go. He lowered his head, and I stood behind him. Usually, I would put my hand on his shoulder, hold his waist, or let him know that I felt his sadness for his mom. But with the gun around his shoulder, I didn't make a move.

"My mother," he said, breaking the silence. "She was a beautiful person, at least that's what I remember. Who knows, though, maybe it’s not. Maybe that's just my brain telling me that, making up memories of the woman I would like her to be. It makes things easier, though, thinking she was a good person, like you."

“Mike,” I said, taking a step closer. “I know in my heart your mother was a good person.”

He shook his head, and glanced at me before

looking down at the tree. "She spent so much time with me at the cabin, singing songs, coloring with me. Dad would always be doing his own thing. I thought we were a happy family. The marks on my mother's wrist – I always stared at them. I thought she'd just hurt herself somehow. I used to call her bruises on her hand boo-boos." He let out a singular laugh.

Mike smiled. "I didn't realize that the marks on her wrist were made by the handcuffs. I didn't understand that my dad had been keeping her at the cabin, against her will. What's happening to Amber right now... is what happened to my mother, but much worse. She was stuck for years." He shook his head. "You knew my parents weren't married. I've told you that. But I never told you that they were never romantically together as well." He let out a sigh. "She was a stranger to my father when he found her, took her, and kept her in the butcher room. It was something he had likely done before. I never asked my dad how many. I knew better. My mom was different, though. He... wanted a family, but who could ever love someone like him?" He turned to me, and I looked away. I knew where the story was going now. "He raped her, and I was born out of that. A year after, she gave birth to Rick... She was forced to have us."

Mike paused. His eyes blazed with a fiery intensity, reflecting the inner rage that was clearly boiling within him.

"I was six years old. I was playing with Rick, with some toys that we had, if you could call them toys. Dad had made them, whittled from wood. Mom was in the kitchen preparing supper when Dad walked up to her and said they had to go for a hike... He told us to say goodbye to Mother, but we were too busy playing with our toys... Rick was too young. I was too naive. I didn't even kiss her or hug my mom goodbye. I barely looked up at her and I waved." A tear welled in Mike's eye and slowly rolled down his cheek. "'I love you, Michael,' my mom said to me before she left. My dad aggressively shoved her out the door... That was the last time I saw her alive."

Mike paused again and I felt my heart sink.

"When my father came back alone, without my mother behind him, I knew something was wrong. I didn't understand. Rick and I cried that night, non-stop. We wanted our mother. We wanted to see her. Where was she? 'She's gone,' Dad said. 'Gone, and she's not coming back.' I didn't understand why. Eventually Rick stopped crying. But I knew something was wrong even at that age. I continue to press my dad. 'Where's Mom? Where is she?' I struck him in the hip out of anger. He grabbed me forcefully by my face. I can still feel how much my cheeks hurt from his strong hands. It felt like my head would be crushed. 'You want to see your mother?' he said. I nodded, trying to shove his hand off my face, failing. He told me to follow him. He told me we were going to go on a hike... Those words scared me. Mom, she went for a hike and never returned, but he said he would bring me to her. When I agreed, he let go of my face. He picked up Rick, grabbed a couple toys, put him in a bedroom and locked the door. He grabbed me forcefully by the hand and pulled me outside. He walked, and walked, and finally he brought me here. To this fallen tree, where he knew mom liked to take us."

"What did he do to her?" I asked, my voice trembling.

"I told you she left... but that's not the truth. He did exactly what he said he would do. He brought me to... her." He pointed at the snow-covered ground. "Right here is where her body was. I still remember her face, and how frightened she seemed even after death. Her lifeless eyes stared at me. The bullet hole in the center of her forehead wasn't easy to miss. It wasn't her blood, or the hole in Mother's head that scared me, though. It was her dead, scared eyes that stared back at me."

Mike looked back down at the fallen tree and then covered his face. More tears fell from his eyes.

The way he spoke, and with my imagination, I could picture the scene easily. I saw my husband, a boy, weeping for his dead mother. I saw Albert Nelson, content at having brought his son to see her.

I felt a tear fall freely from my own eyes

now. What a terrible sight for a young boy to see. I pictured Junior finding my body, and couldn't stop crying. "I'm sorry, Mike," I said. "I never knew your father..."

"Don't talk about him," he said sternly. "I hated my father that day. If I'd had a weapon I would have killed him and left him for the animals, like he did with my mother. Like we had done with so many others." Mike turned to me, weeping. He took a step forward and brushed my tears away with his hand. "Do not cry for me, please. I don't deserve them… Despite my anger, my rage, I became him. Just like him."

"Why are you telling me all of this?"

"Nine women," he answered. "That's how many … How many I killed. Nine young girls, just like Amber. I found a girl at their most vulnerable. I kidnapped them with Rick, and my father. Eventually they died by my hand."

"I don't want to hear this!" I shouted.

He shook his head. "You need to hear this! You need to know it all now."

"You're scaring me. I don't want to know about what you did in the past. I don't—"

"You were supposed to be the tenth," he interrupted, staring at me intently. "That day, at Crescent Lake. you were all by yourself. I knew you were going to be my next victim. My tenth. And then... your accident happened. I don't know what came over me. I… had this urge to do something.

Help you. When I took you out of the lake and on to the dock, you were beautiful. I became instantly infatuated by you. When you came to and were able to talk to me, I knew things were different. I told Rick. I told my father. I wasn't going to hurt you. And then, soon we started dating, and eventually, we built our life together... I couldn't do it anymore, damn it. I didn't want to. My father and Rick told me I was stupid. They told me women are good for nothing. They told me you would just break my heart. My father said I didn't need women for more than what we used them for. A woman would just make me soft, he said. 'If you raise a child with a woman, your son will be a wimp. Not strong. Pray to God you don't have a daughter with her,' he warned me, but I didn't care. None of that mattered because I loved you so much. I still... love you. But none of that matters either, because now you know."

"Mike... stop," I said, turning away from him.

"I was depressed for the past while. I worried this would happen. That you would see me for who I was. I was angrier at myself, for the things I've done. I wish none of it happened. Junior is now the age I was when I lost my mother...There's no turning back from this, though. You know everything. There's no pretending. I'm not the man you thought I was. I'm not the man you fell in love with. I'm... terrible. Rotten. I'm a monster, Dawn.

You're the actress, but I've been pretending to be something I'm not for our whole relationship. Hell, I even fooled myself for some time." Mike took the rifle from his shoulder and raised it towards my chest. "I was naive to think that this wouldn't end up this way." A tear rolled off his chin to the cold snow below. "I never thought I could ever find a woman who would love me. I didn't think I was capable of being loved. I didn't think that was possible. I wish it wasn't. I wish we never happened." Mike lowered the gun.

"Stop," I shouted. "You don't have to do this. What about Junior? What about us? Our family?"

"I wish there was another way, but there isn't. It all ends, now."

I lowered my head. Amber Townsin was wrong. Mike's love was not enough to keep me alive. All the acting I'd done this weekend with Mike had been for nothing. I'd pretended that Mike's dream of the three of us living at the cabin could work, while scheming of ways to escape. I felt a flicker of anger thinking of Amber, approaching me in the basement, blaming me for everything that was happening to her. She was angry at me for not saving her, despite my life now coming to an end. She was wrong about everything.

Mike knew his plan wasn't going to work, because he couldn't trust me. All of our trust issues were because of Amber.

"Stop." I raised my hands and closed my eyes,

waiting for the blast. When I opened my eyes, the barrel of his rifle was pointed at my forehead. I took a deep breath. "I'll kill her myself."

Mike stared at me. "What do you mean?"

"It's the only way this can work," I said, lowering my hands. "I'll kill Amber myself. That's what this is about... Trust. You can trust me. If I kill her, I'll earn yours, maybe even Rick's."

"You couldn't," Mike said, shaking his head. "You're not like me. You're not a bad person. You're a—"

"Victim?" I said, finishing his sentence. "Not when it comes to my family. For you, for Junior, I'd gladly kill her. Give me a gun, and let's start our new life."

CHAPTER 37

Amber

The darkness of the basement was suffocating. I lay awake, listening to the sound of footsteps above me. Three pairs of footsteps. I knew one of them belonged to Rick, the man who had captured me and locked me in this underground prison. The other, his brother Mike, who seemed just as capable of being a monster.

I couldn't sleep, not with the constant fear of what they might do to me.

All I had to keep me comfortable were my thoughts, which were not comforting in the least. They were of my captors visiting me in the basement. I saw them... hurting me. Fulfilling whatever plans they had yet to complete.

I was, after all, Mike's birthday gift, Rick had said. He planned to sacrifice me to his brother to appease whatever bloodlust the sick bastard had.

I thought of my mother. What would she do after I was gone? Would she somehow know I was no longer alive? I had heard of mother's intuition.

Or, worse, would my mother not give up hope that I would come back to her someday?

I couldn't imagine a worse feeling.

The night we escaped my father, I demanded she call the cops. I shouted at her to report him. I didn't realize what she meant, even though it was a plain sentence.

"Bad guys get away," she told me. It was better for us to put my father and what he did behind us. My mom told me it was better to move on than to expect justice in an unjust world.

I didn't believe her. I knew she was wrong. I was naive to think I was right. I went as far as to want to be a lawyer to prove her wrong. I would show her, force her to see it for herself.

The bad men in this world wouldn't get away from me.

Now, as I heard the footsteps above me, I knew she was right. She was right about everything.

"I'm sorry, Mom," I whispered to myself. I wished her intuition was real, so that she could hear my apology. Let those be the last words she heard from me, rather than the hateful ones I gave her.

I sat with my thoughts as the night dragged on. The pairs of footsteps became only one after a while. That pair began walking across the room, and descending the stairs. I knew it was Rick, and a chill ran down my spine. The door creaked open, and there he was, standing in the doorway with a sinister smile on his face. He didn't wear his wolf mask this time, and without it, he seemed even more terrifying. In his hand, he held a bowl of dog food and another of water, which he placed on the floor.

I stared at him wide-eyed, waiting for him to do something. He didn't say a word to me. He only smiled. I tried to keep my distance from him, but he walked towards me, closing in. I backed away, but there was nowhere to go. He stopped in the middle of the room, gazing down at me as I cowered against the cement wall. He reached up and pulled on a string, and turned off the light, leaving me in complete darkness except for the dim glow filtering in from the stairs. I could still see his twisted grin as he walked out of the room.

"Goodnight, girl," he said with a laugh, and slammed the door shut behind him.

I felt my rage bubble over, and screamed. Eventually my anger simmered until it turned to tears.

"Tough girl," I whispered to myself, and shook my head. That was what my father had called me. He liked how feisty my temperament was. He proudly told his friends that he had a tough little girl.

I had to be tough to make it in my house. I had to put on a strong face to let him think I wasn't weak. I had to pretend I was strong, and not scared to death that the blows he struck Mom would come to me.

Even when my mother escaped from him, I continued to wear my tough girl costume.

My stomach grumbled with hunger. I had barely eaten all day. Even in the darkness I could smell the meal my captor left for me. The aroma of dog food filled the room as I tried to find the bowl. When my foot nudged against the cold steel, I took a deep breath. I hated myself for what I was about to do.

I took my time lowering myself until I could take a bite. The kibble tasted as terrible as you would think it would. The dry bits crumbled in my mouth. I struggled with swallowing the bland pieces. It tasted like a dry and salty cereal that had expired.

Tough girl?

I thought I was one. Now, as I ate dog food, trapped in the basement, I knew I wasn't anything more than what the Master wanted me to be. I was just another victim. Beholden to the man of the house.

I thought of my father again, another tear welling in my eye. I moved my body around until I felt the bowl of water. I took my time sipping from it. Eventually, I had to use the bucket. It was everything my captor, Rick, would love to see.

It took a long time for me to be able to pull down my pants and relieve myself into it. Without toilet paper, it felt disgusting putting my clothes back on, which took even longer to do with my hands bound behind me.

I searched for the table, and eventually found it, but it was too difficult to climb up on. All I wanted was to sleep this nightmare away. Eventually, I gave up trying to sleep on the table, and lay on the cold cement floor, and forced my eyes shut. I woke up several times, unsure if it was morning or not. I wondered what Rick was doing upstairs. What he and Mike had planned for me next.

I thought of Dawn. She wasn't in the basement with me, but she was still trapped. I took a deep breath, hating myself for the words I'd told her before she was removed by her husband.

I was angry. I wanted someone to blame, and Dawn was an easy target. The wife of one of my captors. The wife of the man who planned to kill me. I closed my eyes again and breathed in deep, managing to fall asleep again, until I heard it.

Footsteps above me. It was morning time, I knew. Eventually, I heard two pairs of footsteps leaving the cabin. After some time, I heard a third pair coming down the stairs.

I knew who it was, of course.

When Rick opened the door, a fresh grin was plastered on his face, illuminated by the light from the stairs. He walked up to me. I struggled to get to my feet and tripped on myself, falling back down to the floor. He stood over me and he pulled on the string above his head, putting on the light. He kept one hand behind his back.

"Good morning," he said with a playful tone. "We're in for a fun day. Another beautiful day. You know you caused me a lot of stress. You were supposed to be my brother's present." He smirked. "Looks like I might just have to open the present up for myself." He showed me the large knife that he'd concealed behind him.

"I'm sorry," I said in a low voice. I looked up at him. "I'm sorry... Master."

He took a step back, his eyebrows raised with a joyful, surprised expression to match. His smile grew wider. He glanced at the near-empty bowl of dog food.

"Oh, you had a meal, too, didn't you, girl," he said with another snicker.

I stood up, taking my time. "Thank you," I whispered. "I'm still hungry, though. Can I have more?"

"No," he answered sternly. "That was your last meal."

I turned my head, not allowing him to see my fear. "I have to use the bucket... I have to go to the bathroom. Can I go, Master?"

He laughed again. "Of course, of course. Go ahead." He didn't turn his head and watched me intently.

I breathed deeply and squatted over the

bucket. Instead of pulling down my pants, I grabbed the top of the bucket. I yelled as I stood up and swung it as hard as I could in his direction.

He screamed as the contents landed on his face and on his person. "You bitch!"

He wiped my solids from his face and raised the knife towards me. Before he could take out his revenge, I ran from the room. Then up the stairs, nearly losing my balance with my hands cuffed. He followed behind me. When I glanced back at him, I tripped on a stair and fell face first. I grimaced in pain as I felt my nose smash into the wooden stairs. I could feel blood gush from my nostrils.

Rick grabbed me by the arm and pulled me up the stairs, tossing me to the floor. He stood over me, his clothes damp with my liquids. I couldn't help but giggle at my powerful captor being humiliated.

"Stop laughing!" he shrieked. "You bitch! I've had enough of you." He took the knife in his hand and pointed it tip-down.

Before he could slice into me, the front door swung open, and Mike and Dawn rushed in. Mike's eyes widened when he saw us.

"Stop!" he shouted.

CHAPTER 38

Dawn

As we opened the cabin door, Rick was standing over Amber, a large knife in his hand. The blade glinted in the dim light as he raised it high, ready to strike. Amber's screams echoed in the silence; her face contorted in fear. But Rick's eyes were glazed over, a mad determination in them.

Mike ran to his brother, and shouted for him to stop, nearly too late. Rick looked at his brother before turning his rage back at Amber, trying to stab her, but Mike tackled him.

“Stop!” he shouted at Rick. “Not yet! We need to talk about this." Mike steadied his voice, yet with a hint of urgency.

"What are you talking about?" Rick said, low and menacing. He slowly got up from the floor. His clothes were damp, and even from across the room I could smell him. "Why isn't she dead?" He pointed his knife at me. "That's what we talked about. What are you doing, brother?"

"Just go clean yourself up. I'll bring Amber

downstairs."

Rick shook his head. "She's dead!" he shouted, pointing at Amber. "And she's dead," Rick said, pointing at me.

I could feel my heart pounding in my chest, my mind racing. Rick's gaze never left me, the knife still in his hand as he walked closer and closer. I could feel my body starting to shake, the fear consuming me.

But then Mike intervened once again. "Go clean yourself up," he said again, his voice stern and commanding. Rick hesitated for a moment, his eyes still locked on mine, before turning and storming off to the bathroom.

As the sound of the running water filled the cabin, Mike said, "This is going to be difficult to negotiate now. Now's not a time to do anything funny. Let me talk to Rick. We can work this out."

He pulled on Amber's shoulder, yanking her from the floor.

"Does that go for me too?" Amber said with a smirk. "Too bad I don't have another bucket!" She spat in Mike's face. My husband's eyes turned cold, and his gait stiffened. For a moment I thought he would strike her.

Instead he wiped his face with his sleeve. He didn't respond to her, but forcefully hauled her back down the stairs. Amber screamed all the way until I heard him shut the butcher room door. She still yelled, her voice now muffled, but her curse words for Rick and Mike were clear.

Mike walked up the stairs slowly. When he got to the top, he stared at me, his eyes intense.

“When do I do it?” I asked.

“Right away,” Mike said. “Rick will demand it.”

I nodded. "Let me do this, for us, for Junior... And we'll be equals again. But,” I said, raising a finger, “you can never do this again. Not with another woman. Not with anybody."

"I never wanted to do this again. It was never my idea." He turned towards the hall, listening to the shower, his expression remorseful. “Stay here,” he said calmly. “I need to get Rick on board with this.”

“You can do it. I know you can.”

Mike walked to the bathroom door, opening it slightly. As he talked to Rick, I sat at the kitchen table, my mind in a whirl. On the table was Rick's backpack, his water bottle strapped to the side. The backpack was open, and I leaned forward, noticing his EpiPen inside. My thoughts were interrupted by the sound of raised voices from the bathroom.

I couldn't make out the exact words, but the tone was clear. Rick was furious, demanding that Amber be killed, while Mike was trying to reason with him. I sat there, frozen in fear and uncertainty, not knowing what the outcome would be.

As their voices raised, there was no

uncertainty about the words.

"You want to keep her alive?" Rick said. "What are you thinking?”

“Dawn’s going to kill her!”

“Dawn’s going to kill Amber?" Rick laughed loudly. “She doesn’t have it in her to kill that woman. That girl. How blind are you? See what that girl downstairs did to me. There’s no way that I'm not killing her!"

“No,” Mike demanded sternly. "You started this. I never asked you to kidnap her. And then you brought Dawn into this. My family, Rick, you brought my family into this.”

“I'm your family, dammit!" Rick shouted. “You knew Dawn would find out about you eventually, and that day has come!”

I sat at the table and covered my face as I heard my fate discussed.

“This wasn’t Dawn’s fault!” Mike yelled.

"I didn't know she had something planned at the cabin! Don’t blame me for wanting to do something special for you!”

"Enough!” Mike shouted. “Dawn is going to kill Amber. If she can do that, she'll prove herself to be trustworthy. She'll prove herself to be able to keep her mouth shut."

I opened my eyes and shook my head. This isn’t going to work, I thought. Rick will never agree. On the counter beside me was the plate of cookies I’d baked, nearly empty. I grabbed one of the ones with nuts, devouring the whole cookie in a few seconds. I grabbed another one, staring at Rick's backpack. I only had a few moments to act.

The sound of the shower turning off brought me back to reality, and I heard Rick's footsteps as he stormed out of the bathroom, a towel around his waist. I prayed they hadn't noticed me.

"Okay, so let me get this straight," Rick yelled. "Dawn kills the girl, and suddenly we can trust her with what our family has done at this cabin?"

"That's right," Mike said, clenching his fist. "That's exactly what will happen."

Rick looked at me and back at his brother, nodding reluctantly. "I'll give you one last try, brother... But if she can't handle it, I'll have a gun on her. And I'll put both of them down... If you don't agree to that, then I don't agree to your terms."

There was silence for a moment. Mike turned and stared at me as he answered. "If Dawn doesn't kill the girl, you have my permission to kill her."

CHAPTER 39

Amber

Locked in the butcher room again, I continued to laugh and scream. The look on Rick's face with my piss and shit over him would be a permanent memory, for however long I was capable of having them. The thought of his disgust and rage after what I did made me want to belly laugh.

He would have killed me if it wasn't for Mike and Dawn. After some time, my hilarity ended. I knew the end of my story was coming. I thought of the torture they could have in store for me. Perhaps what I did to Rick could provide me with a quick death. Anything was better than staying in the basement. I couldn't handle it anymore.

I heard footsteps coming down the stairs and the door opened. Rick, with a new change of clothes on, stared at me. This time he didn't smile.

"Time to go," he said, his eyes full of rage. Before I could say anything, he ran over to me, grabbed me forcefully, with my arms behind my back, and pulled me up the stairs.

"No more witty comments," he said. I tried to lean back, so that he would fall with me down the stairs but he positioned himself better and held me tighter. "No more buckets. No more fun," he grumbled. "This is it."

I stopped fighting, knowing there wasn't much else I could do. I thought of my life. I thought of my mom, and how I didn't tell her I loved her before I was taken. I thought of my time at university. The last several years I'd been studying non-stop to be a lawyer. To protect others from people like Rick. I wished I had done anything else. I could have travelled more. Made more memories. If I wasn't at university, I wouldn't have been kidnapped to begin with.

I smirked.

"What's so damn funny, girl?" Rick said, pausing a moment and holding me up against the narrow stairwell wall.

I laughed again. "Irony," I said.

"Irony?" Rick repeated through clenched teeth. "What do you mean?"

"It'll go over your head. Like explaining algebra to an ant. You're going to get away with this, I know."

Now, Rick smirked. "Upstairs," he said, pushing me one last step.

The bad guys get away. They were wise words that I should have listened to.

Now on the main floor, I saw that Mike and Dawn were already dressed and changed into their winter clothes, boots, and jackets. Rick grabbed his backpack from the table and swung it around his shoulder. He grabbed his rifle from the counter and pushed me towards the front door.

"We're going for a little hike, the four of us," he said, smiling at me. "This is not the usual way we do things, so it's a first for me as well. Let's go."

Dawn stared at me quietly and Mike had an emotionless expression. He opened the door and Rick shoved me outside. My socks were wet immediately in the deep snow.

"That way," Rick said, pointing his gun towards a grouping of trees. When I didn't move, he shoved my back with the rifle and I started hiking.

I lead, taking Rick's directions. Trudging through the snow, I glanced back and Mike was beside his brother, walking and talking quietly amongst themselves. Dawn was the last in the pack, her head down.

"Faster," Rick said. "Move along." He walked up to me and shoved me again and I fell into the snow. "Get up!" He grabbed me by my arms, nearly ripping my shoulder out, pulling me to my feet.

The light snow falling was getting heavier. It was near whiteout conditions. After what felt like ages, my body aching from the cold, Mike yelled for me to stop. It felt like a random part of the forest, except for a large fallen tree.

"We're here." Rick smiled. He took his gun and flicked a switch on the top of the scope. A red laser went across the white snow. He moved his gun until the laser focused on me. I looked down and saw the dot directly on my heart. "Today we're going to have a little girl-on-girl action," he said proudly. "Take it away, Dawn." Rick suddenly swung his gun until the red dot was on Dawn's forehead.

She took in a deep breath, knowing Rick's sight was on her, but she didn't run, or scream. She continued to stare at me.

Mike walked up to his wife and handed her his rifle. "Safety's off," he said. "You can do this."

Dawn nodded. "Justice... Your father's rifle."

"This ends with his gun."

Rick took a few steps back from Dawn, aiming at her midsection.

"I'm so sorry," she said, slowly raising the gun towards me.

Rick smirked. "You can do this, sister."

I pursed my lips at Dawn, unable to hide my anger. "I told you you were going to make it out of this," I said to her. "I knew it from the beginning. I knew from the beginning that I was going to be dead, and I knew you would find a way to save yourself!"

"Shut up!" Dawn muttered. "Stop talking."

I shook my head. "Will me shutting up stop you from killing me? Killing me at their command?

Like they wanted you to?"

Dawn took in a deep breath, aiming her weapon. "Actually, this was my idea."

I scoffed. "You were always one of them. Just another wolf in sheep's clothing. Go ahead, then."

"Close your eyes!" she shouted.

I shook my head. "I won't help you with this! I want you to remember my eyes."

Mike took a step forward. "Just do it, Dawn," he said calmly. "Do it for me. Do it for our family. For Junior."

"I'm rooting for you, sister," Rick said with a laugh.

Dawn lowered her head. "I don't know. I don't know if I can do this. I thought... I could."

"That's because you're thinking too much, sister," Rick said. "It's you or her."

Mike put his hand up at Rick. "Just give her a moment. Your first kill was ugly to watch too, Rick."

Rick shook his head. "Tick tock, sister."

Dawn gazed at me, raising the gun again slowly, her mouth open. "I have to do this."

Instead of fear, I felt pity for Dawn. I smiled. "You know they'll kill you next. Maybe not today or tomorrow. Eventually though, they'll take you for a walk, and you'll never come back. You know it, and I know it."

CHAPTER 40

Dawn

Amber's eyes were intense and full of rage, showing no fear as I looked back at her through tears.

"I'm sorry," I repeated, my voice barely audible. My hand was shaking as I held the rifle directly at her. Mike's father's gun felt heavy in my hand, as if it was dragging me down with the weight of what I was about to do.

Rick had his rifle trained on me, the red dot on my jacket taunting me with its eerie glow. I could feel my arm lowering.

With tension at its highest, Rick laughed. "Okay, okay," he said. "I guess that's it."

"Don't shoot her!" Mike yelled.

"Brother, I'd love for this grand plan you have to work out, but it's not going to." Rick glared at me. "You're only making what I have to do harder... If it wasn't for Mike, you both would have been dead last night."

"Stop scaring her!" Mike shouted. "Dawn,

take a moment. Breathe in, and when you breathe out, pull the trigger, okay?"

I nodded at my husband, and raised the gun at Amber again.

Rick snickered. "Sister, I'm a fair guy. I'll give you the cliche count of ten before I shoot." He adjusted his aim, waving the red beam into my face.

"Ten!" Rick shouted.

"Just do it!" Mike screamed at me.

"Nine."

I gazed at Amber, who regarded me coldly. For all my acting skills, I'd failed in the role of a supportive wife of a serial killer. None of my plans had worked. I'd never wanted to kill her. I'd had a plan, and it failed miserably. I still had a choice, though. Pull the trigger. Kill her.

What Amber said felt true, though. Eventually my husband would hold Justice in his hands and point it at me before pulling the trigger.

"Eight!" Rick shouted.

"Get it over with!" Mike shouted. "Please!"

"Seven!"

I thought of a memory of Junior and Mike playing wrestling on the bed. Mike tossed him into a mountain of pillows. They both laughed hysterically.

"Six!"

Another memory played in my mind of Mike and I holding hands, hiking around the family cabin. Junior ran ahead of us on the trail, finding a dead snake and picking it up with a stick, making a yucky face. I yelled for him to put it down but Mike laughed it off. "Boys will be boys," he said.

"Five!" Rick shouted with a harsh tone.

I remembered the date that we had at Crescent Lake. After I was discharged from the hospital from the heart attack, Mike took me there. He called it exposure therapy. I remembered how shy I'd felt around him. We shared our first kiss on the dock as we dipped our toes in the cold water that nearly killed me. How often did you have strong feelings for the man who... saved you?

I glanced at Mike, watching me in horror, as Rick counted down.

"Four!"

"Do it, dammit!" Mike yelled. "Please, I need you."

"Three!"

I thought of Junior and his sweet face. His beautiful smile. I remembered his voice on the phone telling me he loved me. I wanted to see that face again. I wanted to hear him say those words to me. I wanted to hold him tight and tell him the same.

"Two!" Rick shouted louder.

I began crying, lowering the gun. I thought of Mike's face the day I told him I was pregnant. The day we found out we were going to be parents. The day our life changed forever. I thought of Mike and I at the altar, kissing, as I said "I do."

I managed to think of so many loving memories until I heard Rick say the word.

"One!"

CHAPTER 41

I pulled the trigger and closed my eyes. A thunderclap echoed through the scenery. Amber Townsin stood exactly where she had moments before, unharmed.

Rick laughed when I opened my eyes. "You were nowhere near her. You're going to make me do it, aren't you?" he asked me with a smirk. You're going to make me shoot you?" He steadied his aim.

My mouth was wide open, waiting for him to fire.

"It's not fair!" Mike shouted.

Rick turned to him, pointing the laser sight at his own brother. "I've been more than fair given what's happened!"

I weighed up my opportunity. All it would take was for me to swivel quickly and pull the trigger. With any luck it would strike Rick.

Rick caught my glance and smiled. "Try it, sister. Try it."

Mike brushed his chest as if trying to swipe away the laser dot. "Don't you ever point that at me, Rick. Move it now!"

"Do you want to give me a ten count, brother?" Rick said with a snicker. "I should just end this... I told you: you can't send a woman to do a man's job."

Rick moved the sight of his gun back to me.

"Not yet!" Mike shouted. Rick rolled his eyes. "She's never used this weapon before. Hell, she never fired a gun, Rick." Mike turned to me. "Do you want me to help you aim? You just pull the trigger... and this is all over."

"No!" Rick shouted. "That was not the agreement. No help. She needs to do this fully on her own. She needs to pull the trigger; she needs to kill her. This doesn't work any other way." Mike bowed his head in defeat, knowing Rick was right. "Ah! You better not hold this against me, brother. I counted to ten. How many ten counts does she need?" Rick turned to me. "How long will it take for you to see, this won't work!"

"Just one more opportunity, Rick," Mike pleaded. "I'm only asking for one more!"

Rick shook his head. "I'm not exactly holding her back right now, am I?" He sighed. Keeping the rifle glued on me with one hand, he reached around and opened the side of his backpack with the other.

I glanced at Amber, who nudged her head towards Rick, and he noticed.

"I'll kill all of you if you try anything." He sifted through his backpack, taking out a cookie.

"Oh, what do we have here?" He raised it in his hand. "I don't remember putting this scrumptious baked good in here. My favourite kind too, with nuts!" He tossed it against the fallen tree, and it hid beneath the snow where it landed.

I turned away, my eyes newly wet. I was running out of time. Soon, I would have to shoot Amber, or die trying to kill Rick. Both options ended with me dead.

"Nice try, sister," Rick said.

I glanced at Mike, who covered his face and shook his head. When he eventually stared back at me, I didn't recognize my husband.

"That one doesn't have nuts," I said, and looked back at Rick. "It's the ones with the green dye that do."

"Well," Rick said with a sneer, "I don't remember putting any baked goods you made in my pack. That means you did. A little foolish, no? Childish." To Mike, he went on, "She literally thought I would just reach into my bag and eat it. Do you see what she's doing here, brother? Can you now agree that this all ends?"

"Don't do it," Mike said. "Let her kill Amber. Let her kill the girl! And this is all over; all is forgiven. You did try to kill Dawn, right? Can you blame her?"

"She thinks we're stupid! These women are no good. Father told us! You stopped paying attention, but not me."

"Father told us a lot of stuff! Not all of it was right."

"Not about them," Rick said, gesturing towards me. "Tell me, brother, if I walk away, and leave the three of you, and if I let Dawn keep the gun, what do you think your dear wife would do?" Mike lowered his head. "Answer me!" Rick screamed. "What would Dawn do?" Rick kept the rifle on me as he grabbed his water bottle from the side of his pack one-handed. He popped it open, downing its contents.

Mike glanced up at me, his eyes tearing. "Just… do it." He turned his head.

"Mike?" I said in shock.

I waited for Rick to fire. Instead, he lowered the rifle and coughed uncontrollably. He covered his mouth with one hand and brought it to his neck, his other dropping the gun completely. Then he had both hands around his throat as he gasped for air.

"Rick!" Mike yelled.

I quickly turned to my husband and pointed his father's rifle at him. "Don't!" I said. "Just stay there."

I took a few steps backwards to ensure Mike couldn't rush me and grab the rifle. He listened and watched in terror as his brother's throat tightened.

Rick continued to cough. "You. Bitch," he said through labored breaths. "Nuts in the… water."

He lowered himself to the ground, his body

fighting against him. Rick managed to grasp his rifle and move it up towards me. I was too slow. He fired, but the bullet whizzed into the woods. Veins popped on Rick's forehead as he mustered the energy to aim his gun, the laser directly on my midsection.

Mike ran and kicked the rifle from his brother's hand. Rick swore to himself, straining to say anything, then fell to the snow-covered ground, wheezing. Mike glanced at the gun near his foot.

I aimed my rifle at my husband. "Don't! Please... don't."

"I'm not," Mike said calmly. He bent down slowly, grabbing his brother's pack where it had fallen into the snow. He reached in and took out Rick's EpiPen.

"Just let me help him! He's still my brother. He's all I have left now." I took a deep breath. I felt a tear coming down the side of my face.

Mike stabbed the pen into his brother and waited for a response. His brother continued to wheeze and cough and roll around on the ground, trying to take in air. Mike seemed confused. He continued to stab him with the pen.

"It's too late!" I shouted. "I used it already. When you guys were talking in the cabin... It's empty. I'm sorry."

Mike looked at me wide-eyed, then slowly back to his brother, who continued to roll around. After a few last convulsions, he fell motionless.

"He's... dead," Mike said softly. He knelt on the snow beside his brother. His hand caressed the side of Rick's inflamed face.

"You were going to let him kill me," I said, pointing the rifle at Mike. "Even if I had killed Amber, you and I both know eventually either him or you would have had to kill me. I couldn't let that happen, not to Junior." I glanced quickly at Amber, who just stared at us in shock. Mike was now eyeing the gun in the snow again. "Stand up!" I shouted. "Get away from him, and move over." Mike listened. "Where are the keys for the handcuffs?"

"Rick keeps them in his backpack."

I motioned for him to take a few more steps away and grabbed Rick's pack, sorting through it quickly while watching Mike. When I found a small pair of keys, I held them and showed them to my husband, who nodded back at me. I went over to Amber and lowered the gun, taking off her handcuffs. Amber flexed her wrists.

"Thank you," she said. "What do we do now?"

I pointed the rifle at my husband again, my eyes full of rage. "I'll tell you what happens. No more smiling!" Amber looked at me strangely. "No more... acting." I shook my head at Mike. "Nine women? Nine! And I was supposed to be another notch on the bedpost for you." Mike didn't respond, and bowed his head. "No more smiling. No more pretending. No more acting! You're a monster,

Mike. A monster who deserves to die!" I yelled at him. "I should kill you," I said in a soft voice. I felt my eyes water again.

"Do it," he said. "It should... be you. I don't deserve you, I never did... Do it!" He stared at me.

I pointed it at his chest. "I loved you!"

"I love you!" Mike shrieked back.

I began to cry, struggling to maintain my aim. "I can't... do it. He doesn't deserve to live. But I can't kill him," I said to Amber. I gave her the rifle. "Maybe you can do what I can't."

Amber nodded. "Never used one of these," she said, taking in a deep breath.

I gazed out into the trees. The snowfall started to lighten, showing the beautiful scenery.

"You're working towards your law degree, right?" I told Amber. "What does someone get for killing nine women?"

She regarded my husband and raised the gun. "Well, that's nine first degree murders. Nine kidnapping charges. Nine assaults.... and one attempted murder," she said with a smirk. Mike was now staring back at her. "Did you touch the others? Did you r—"

"I did many terrible things. I deserve this."

I covered my mouth in shock. "Kill him," I whispered.

Amber scowled, took a step forward and levelled the gun at his forehead. Mike closed his eyes.

CHAPTER 42

We hiked back to the cabin without saying a word. All I could think about was what I'd left behind in the woods, by the fallen tree.

I thought of Junior, and the image of his face in my mind made me even more sad.

What would I tell him? How much should I tell him?

He was old enough to understand life and death. He understood evil, even if he'd never experienced it himself.

I thought of the Mike I used to know. The husband I had. My partner in life. It was all fake from the very beginning.

Mike was a better actor than me.

At the fallen tree I'd left behind any thoughts that my husband was a good person.

The monster that hiked in front of us back to the cabin was the cruel reality of a man I'd never truly known. Amber had her rifle aimed at him, ready for anything. I'd shouldered his father's gun, trying to not think about the husband I used to have.

As Mike walked ahead of us, Amber and I whispered about what to do now. We were in agreement.

Once inside the cabin, she readied her rifle. "You know where to go," she said to Mike harshly.

Mike nodded and quietly walked into the basement.

"Open the butcher door," I said once we were downstairs. Mike turned to me and I gestured towards the room with his father's rifle.

He opened the door meekly and stared into the dark room, taking in a deep breath.

"You can turn the light on," Amber said. "I never got a choice, but you can."

Mike stepped inside and pulled on the string, illuminating the windowless room. I walked in, picked up the chair and placed it neatly for him. I cleaned up as Amber held her weapon on Mike.

Amber reached into her pocket quickly, and tossed the handcuffs at Mike, who caught them. "You know what to do," she said. Mike fixed his glasses before putting the cuff on his hands.

"Tighter," Amber said, and Mike pushed on the cuffs, clicking them tighter on his wrist until he couldn't.

Mike turned to me. "I'm... sorry."

"Sorry?" I repeated. I looked at him, void of any love I once had. I walked over to the bucket on the floor, picking it up with my sleeve, and turned it over neatly for my husband. "Or, sorry you got caught?"

"None of this was my idea, ever."

Amber pointed the rifle at him. "Right, I'm sure that's what those other nine women thought before you killed them. Or the countless others your father and brother killed after you did nothing to help."

Mike turned to me again, his eyes damp. "What about Junior?"

"He will know. Someday he'll understand what you are."

Mike lowered his head. "Just kill me."

"No," Amber said bluntly. "I'm going to make sure you get something much worse. I'm going to expose you, and your family."

I nodded in agreement. "It's still snowing outside," I said coldly. "Roads are probably blocked at least for the rest of the weekend."

Amber smiled. "Even if we call the cops, they'll struggle to get here." Mike looked at her. For the first time I saw fear.

I stepped outside of the room, and brought back a bowl of water and another with dog food. I placed them beside the bucket.

"Seems like we'll still get to spend your birthday weekend together," I whispered.

EPILOGUE

Amber

Six Years Later

I sat at my desk in the courtroom, waiting for the jury to come back from their quarters with a decision. The judge looked as bored as I had, staring at his phone.

The defense attorney read a book and seemed comfortable. It was almost as if he knew the verdict before the jury announced it.

Despite the defence's confidence, his client, Mr. Antonio Verdie, stared blankly at the door, waiting for the jury of his peers to return.

Guilty or not guilty.

Of course, I knew he was guilty. The evidence was plain for anyone to see. Mr. Verdie had physically assaulted his wife, Christina, on multiple occasions. Christina Verdie, despite being scared for her life, documented the last few altercations they had by taking photos of the bruises her husband made on her.

Hospital reporting told the story of a woman

who fell down the stairs, fracturing her arm in three places. Christina had told the jury the truth though. Antonio did it to her. It wasn't an accident. It was her husband's rage.

With all the evidence piled high, it was hard to think that there was any chance of a not guilty verdict. However, my peers at the crown attorney's office thought there was a good chance of a hung jury.

The reason? Mr. Antonio Verdie was a wealthy and well-known community figure. He paraded through the town with his wife, and many thought they were happily married. No one knew the horrors she endured behind closed doors.

His team of lawyers did their best to portray Christina as a bored housewife who wanted out of a marriage and to take all her husband's money. Christina's closest friend, who testified for the defence, lied that Christina said she wanted to set her husband up to destroy his image. She purposefully hurt herself to document bruises, to blame her husband.

The media portrayed Antonio Verdie as the true victim of this court case, not his money-grubbing wife.

I knew, of course, that was false. What bothered me more was how easily some stood by Mr. Verdie.

How would I react if the jury came back to the courtroom and delivered the news that

Mr. Verdie's expensive, smug lawyer would love to hear?

I breathed in deep, trying not to show my worry. Cameras were always ready to take candid photos of anyone in the room.

My first case as a crown prosecutor could be a complete failure.

None of the other prosecutors wanted this case. Mr. Verdie had supportive members in high places. One of the reasons my colleagues couldn't take the case was conflict of interest. Many had gone to his fundraisers, or schmoozed with him at events, and rubbed elbows with him and his elite friends at parties. It was the reason why many in the city who supported Christina Verdie thought she would never get a fair trial.

Why did I volunteer myself to be humiliated?

I looked to the back of the courtroom. My mother smiled at me. She raised her hand from her lap and waved.

I nodded back with a smile of my own, wishing I hadn't told her today would be the day I found out the outcome of my first trial. It was as if my mother wanted to watch me during my first day of school. She'd asked if it was okay if she came, and I reluctantly agreed.

She sat on the same side as Christina Verdie. Christina sat in the middle of the courtroom, her father's arm around her, comforting her. Christina

Verdie's daughter, Melissa, was not present. The young girl had asked her mother if she could be, but Christina had refused. I wasn't sure if that was because she didn't want her daughter to see her father in such a terrible way, or because she was worried he would get away with what he'd done.

Bad men get away with what they do. I glanced back at my mother. What would have happened if my mother reported what my father had done to her?

Would he have gone free?

If she had reported him, and my father did have a trial, my mother would not have been able to stop me from being in the courtroom when a jury read his verdict. No judge would have stopped me from cheering, watching my father get the justice he deserved.

I took a deep breath. He got away though. He never got what he deserved.

I thought of the cabin. I thought of the basement. Those memories still haunted me at times. What made it better, though, was knowing that the Nelson brothers didn't get away.

Rick's verdict had been swift and merciless, at the hands of Dawn. Mike's was a much slower process, but justice nonetheless.

Mike Nelson would rot in a jail cell for the rest of his life. Life without the possibility of parole.

Despite media demanding an interview with the sole remaining member of the Nelson family murderers, Mike refused any attention. That didn't stop crime channels making docuseries and writers speculating on what happened, or even Hollywood.

I understood a movie would be coming out in the near future. I was excited to find out who would play me.

It was weird to say, but I had many fans now. Women around the world loved the resilient character they heard about in the news or saw on television shows recreating what happened. A feisty kidnapped woman, who fought with everything she could against her captors. I enjoyed watching the actors in a recent true crime show play out when I tossed the bucket full of excrement at Rick in the basement.

Even though I hated the attention myself, I couldn't deny the power it had over my career. After my story was told to the world, the local crown attorney's office gave me an employment offer before I had even graduated or finished my bar exams.

After what happened at the Nelson family cabin, forensic teams scoured the property and wilderness. Scuba divers were sent to Crescent Lake. In total they found the remains of over thirty-seven different women. DNA helped identify some, but many remained nameless.

More troubling, though, was Mike Nelson's own testimony he provided willingly, which suggested there were likely many more women never found.

The thought of Rick and Mike Nelson made me think of Dawn. We had kept in touch for a while. Over the years, though, I found it difficult to continue any ongoing communication with her. It was a reminder of a time I wished to forget about entirely.

Recently, a reporter had approached me and said that Dawn was starting to let her son talk to Mike again with visitations at prison. The reporter wanted my thoughts on this. I politely refused to give any comment.

Although I wanted nothing more than to forget about what happened at the Nelson cabin, some couldn't escape it. I felt sad for Dawn's little boy, who was much older now.

No matter how terrible his father was, he still wanted him in his life.

I didn't know how I felt about that, but that wasn't my decision to make.

The door swung open and the jury returned to their seats. Everyone stood. The judge confirmed a verdict had been made.

After it was read, my mouth gaped. My heart raced. I nearly joined the small crowd who cheered.

"Guilty."

I looked to the back of the courtroom and shared a smile with my mother.

◆◆◆

Note from the author:

I truly hope you enjoyed reading my story as much as I did creating it. As an indie author, what you think of my book is all I care about.

If you enjoyed my story, please take a moment to leave your review on the Amazon store. It would mean the world to me.

Thank you for reading, and I hope you join me next time.

Download My Free Book

If you would like to receive a FREE copy of my psychological thriller, The Affair, please email me at jamescaineauthor@gmail.com.

Alice Ruffalo is on the run from her violent husband. She believes she found safety in a rundown motel in a small town.

The handsome motel clerk helps take her mind off her fears, until she starts to hear weird sounds outside her motel room and sees shadowy figures near her door.

Alice finds out the hard way that she shouldn't have stopped in this small town. Her husband knows exactly where she is.

⭑⭑⭑⭑⭑ *"This is such a thrilling read." Goodreads reviewer*

⭑⭑⭑⭑⭑ "A brilliant read. " Goodreads reviewer

I'm always happy to receive
emails from readers at
jamescaineauthor@gmail.com.

Thanks again,
James

THE IN-LAWS

She visited them for the weekend. Now they won't let her leave.

Chelsea Jameson married the perfect husband, but he doesn't like to talk about his past.

She finds out why when his parents invite them to stay at their off-the-grid cabin in the woods.

His mother dominates his life, even though her only son is in his thirties. Her mother-in-law creates conflict and tries to manipulate her husband against Chelsea.

When Chelsea discovers more about her husband's parents, dark family secrets are unearthed, revealing the truth. This is not a regular visit to the in-laws.

Isolated and in the middle of nowhere, Chelsea needs to play their game if she wants to survive her visit.

The In-Laws is a page-turning psychological thriller that will have you guessing till the very end.

Please enjoy this sneak preview of The In-Laws:

◆◆◆

Chapter One

Martha Jameson looked one last time in Henry's room, satisfied that everything was perfect for her *son* to return to. He was finally coming home after such a long time. Everything had to be perfect when he visited.

Martha smiled. She missed him. He barely came to visit now that he was older. He has visited even less since *she* came into the picture.

Beside the bed on the nightstand was a picture of her. Chelsea. His *wife*. She had long blond hair, and large blue eyes. The picture was of her in a long-sleeved white shirt. She's only twenty-one and beaming with beauty. She's gorgeous and from what Henry says her soul is even more beautiful. This only angered Martha more. She turned the frame face down.

Martha looked across the room at a different

picture frame on the dresser. She picked it up and stared at it. Martha was in her thirties when the photo was taken, and Henry was much younger. Her hand was wrapped around his shoulder. They were both smiling.

Those were different times though. Things are *different* now.

She moved the picture frame and placed it on his nightstand, replacing his wife's photo. She picked up the other frame of Chelsea and moved it to the dresser.

"Martha!" She heard his raspy voice calling for her but did not answer. She was caught up thinking about how things *used* to be. "Martha! Where are you?"

"Henry's room!" she called out to her husband. Arthur limped into the room. He grimaced in pain when he stood beside her. "Leg hurting again?" she asked.

"It's the moisture in this old home," Arthur said, sitting on Henry's bed. He made a sound of relief when he did. "Mornings are getting harder."

Martha scoffed. "I just made his bed; get off!"

He nodded and stood up, grimacing again. Arthur coughed into his flannel sleeve. 'What time are they coming?"

"Should be around supper."

Arthur cleared his throat. "Good. I need more time to get ready."

"Finish in the garden first," Martha said

sternly. When she didn't hear Arthur respond, she turned to him with a cold glare. Her husband was staring off into the room. She snapped her finger at him. "Are you going to be *ready* for Henry? For— his wife? Don't mess this up."

Arthur cleared his throat and pushed his disheveled gray hair to the side. "I won't."

"We need to keep our stories straight, right?"

"Right, Martha. Of course." He wrinkled his nose and stared off into the room again to Martha's dismay.

Martha sighed. "What's her name? Do you even remember?"

Arthur cleared his throat. "Chelsea."

Martha wasn't impressed. "You're going to mess this up for us. I know it." Before her husband could respond she barked another order. "*Go*. Finish your work in the yard. I'll clean the house some more and get a salad ready from the garden for them."

Arthur didn't react as he left the room. She watched her husband limp on his left leg as he went down the hall. Time had not been kind to him. He was only sixty-five, but his body was that of a seventy-five-year-old.

Martha went down the hallway and stared out the front window. How much longer could Arthur stay out here? She had lived off the grid forever. They had their own garden, septic system, and solar panels. There were repairs to complete, maintenance tasks to stay ahead of. Could Arthur handle this lifestyle much longer? When Henry came, she would talk to him more about it.

Martha noticed a pile of white fluff surrounded by green grass outside. It was hard for her to make the white blur out, but it appeared to be moving. She took out her glasses from her dress pocket to take a closer look.

"Damnit," she said. "Not again." She tightened her lower lip as she looked at the dying chicken on the grass. She made her way outside the cabin. The grass surrounding the bird was stained with blood and feathers. The chicken moved its wings slowly. Martha picked it up by its neck and put it out of its misery with a twist.

She followed the path towards the barn where Arthur was already shoveling topsoil into a patch of small plants.

He looked at Martha and wiped the sweat from his forehead. "Chicken tonight?" He laughed to himself.

Martha was not amused. She raised its body to his face, dangling it rigorously. "That wolf is back! Set up some traps when you're done here."

He nodded. "Sure." He dug his shovel into the wheelbarrow full of soil and sprinkled it over the small plants. "Tomatoes are going to come in nicely I think."

"That wolf is going to *ruin* everything," Martha said, ignoring his comment.

“I’m almost done here,” he said. “I’ll put out a few traps. It’s been weeks since we saw it. It will move on again.”

Martha looked down at the tomato plants. They were sprouting nicely as he said. Then she noticed a dirty finger sticking out from the ground beside a leafy plant. She shook her head as she saw several other fingers from the hand sprouting out from the soil.

“No wonder why the wolf is back,” she barked, pointing at the fingers. She looked closely at one finger. An emerald ring was clearly visible on one of the blue-hued digits. Martha bent over and wrestled it off. She rubbed dirt off the band with her fingers, and spit. “You need to do a better job, Arthur,” she said sternly. “Henry is coming with his wife. It needs to be perfect.”

Arthur nodded, stuck his shovel in the wheelbarrow, and covered the hand with dirt until it was fully hidden.

Martha smiled thinly. If things are perfect Henry will never want to leave again.

Chapter Two

Chelsea looked out the passenger side window, taking in the woods and mountains surrounding them as Henry drove off the highway into a gas station.

"You still have half a tank," Chelsea said to her husband with a smile. "Aren't we getting close to your parents by now?" It had already been over a two-hour drive from their apartment in Calgary.

Henry smirked. "First rule: when you live out in the middle of nowhere, always gas up when you can because you may not be able to until it's too late. Learned that lesson the hard way a few times when I was younger."

Henry parked his pickup truck in front of the gasoline pump. He turned off the ignition and smirked at Chelsea again. "How about I pump, and you go inside and get a few snacks for the rest of our road trip. Grab a few of those junkie gas station brownies too, I love those. Maybe a few for my parents."

"I thought your parents lived off the land. What do they need gas bar junk brownies for?"

"They taste delicious, that's all that matters. Pretty please, sweetheart." He opened the driver side door and got out, grabbing the gas pump.

Chelsea got out of his truck and stretched her legs. She looked around at the lonely gas station on the empty road. They truly were in the middle of nowhere.

"How much longer until we get to your parents?" she asked.

Henry opened the gasket but sighed to himself as he put the pump back on the hook. "I'm getting used to the city now. They don't have pay at the pump options out here. When you go inside, can you ask them for $30 on the pump as well?"

"Sure," she said.

"And: about another hour and a half or two," he answered her with a grin.

Chelsea turned to walk towards the gas bar, but Henry whistled at her. She turned and he raised his wallet. "You may need this," he said. Chelsea put out her hand, but he waved for her to get closer, smiling.

"Stop playing games with me, Henry," she said with a laugh. "My back hurts and I want junkie gas station gummy bears as much as you want brownies." He didn't answer but kept waving her over to him.

When she was close enough, he grabbed her and pushed her against the side of the truck. He kissed her softly and leaned against her body. She could feel how *excited* he was already.

"There's something about being in the middle of nowhere with you that makes me want to tear your clothes off." he said, biting his lip.

"Stop," Chelsea said shyly. "Let's gas up, *first*."

She kissed him.

He stepped back and raised her left hand, kissing her wedding band. “As you wish. Don’t make me wait too long. I’m hungry… for *brownies*.”

Chelsea shoved him. “You’re trouble.” She leaned in and kissed him again. Butterflies fluttered in her stomach every time she kissed her handsome husband.

The *honeymoon stage*, some call it. They had only been married for a few months and could barely keep their hands off each other. Even though Henry was thirty-four, he took good care of his body, and was successful, charming and funny. Sometimes Chelsea didn’t understand what he saw in her. She was almost the complete opposite.

“Need gas?” an older, stockier man called out to them from the gas bar entrance. He stared at them awkwardly. “You have to pay inside.”

“Sorry!” Chelsea yelled back. “Be right there.”

“Why are you apologizing?” Henry whispered, raising his wallet higher.

“Stop it,” Chelsea said back. “Give me the wallet.” She looked back and the man was still staring at them. “He’s watching.”

“So what?” Henry said with a laugh.

“*Please*… give me the wallet?”

Henry lowered his hand. “Fine, I’m done playing around.”

Chelsea snatched it from his hand, and when she turned to walk to the store, Henry smacked her butt. Chelsea looked back at him with an irritated face. She hated public affection like that. It was what others thought about it that bothered her most. As soon as she saw Henry's face, though, she felt nothing but his love.

“For that,” she said, “I’m buying some potato chips too!” She walked towards the store and the old man went back inside the gas bar behind the counter.

She was amazed at how rustic everything was at the station. She spotted a phone booth beside the building and chuckled to herself. She couldn't remember the last time she saw a functional phone booth. She thought about going inside the booth and calling Henry from it to mess with him but decided the old man at the gas station had been waiting long enough for his only customers of the day.

When she went inside, she greeted the man behind the till, but he didn't respond. She went into the chip aisle and grabbed a few bags. She took her time going through the rest of the junk food aisle and spotted some gummy bears. Above them were the infamous brownies Henry had been craving. She grabbed a few bags and brought everything to the counter.

“Can I have thirty worth of gas, please, as well?” she asked.

The old man punched keys on his register and looked at her. “Forty-five,” he said with a nasty tone. It was if her shopping in his store, with no other customers, was bothersome to him.

His curtness bothered her more. How many customers had he had today, being in the middle of nowhere? He can't smile or greet his customers? Thank them for saving his business? Instead of that happening, she paid the bill and thanked *him*.

She thought about what Henry said about the trip being another two hours potentially. She glanced around the small gas bar, looking for a washroom.

"Anything else?" the man asked.

"Is there a washroom here?"

Instead of answering he pointed at a sign. "The Outhouse is for paying customers only." Below the sign was a hook with a key on it.

"When you're done using it, lock the door," he said.

"Never mind," Chelsea said with a smile. "Thanks." She turned to leave and saw a billboard beside the exit door. Although the board was small it was stacked with missing persons posters. Some were piled on top of each other.

Chelsea glanced at a few posters. It amazed her to think all the pictures of the people on this board were missing. Someone out there was looking for them and they couldn't be found. How many of them were alive? How many were only runaways, who wanted to stay missing for their own reasons? She hoped for most of these people it was the latter.

She noticed a weathered poster tacked underneath two others. Caroline Sanders. She had been missing for over two years. Last seen hiking the Grassi Lakes Trail in Kananaskis Country. At the bottom of the page was a case number and phone number to call with any information.

Chelsea took her time looking at the rest of the board at all the missing faces staring back at her. Most of them were older men and women, with a few exceptions.

"Do you want to buy some lottery tickets?" the old man asked.

"What?" Chelsea said.

The old man nodded at the lottery station below the missing persons board. "Just fill out your lucky numbers and maybe you could be the next one who wins. You saw that winning ticket on the board?"

Chelsea looked up at the board again. Below the posters of a few women was a picture of a lottery ticket. Handwritten, with poor lettering, were the words "$25,000 Winner."

"That could be you," the old man said with an ugly leer.

Chelsea was annoyed. The board of these missing people was desecrated with this man's greed. No wonder the missing stay vanished.

"I'm not that lucky," Chelsea said. She left the store without saying goodbye to the cashier.

To her that was the worst thing she could do to someone, leave without acknowledging them. To the old man, he could care less if he ever saw her again – or if her face was on the bulletin board some day.

"Excuse me, miss." Chelsea turned to see a young boy with pudgy cheeks on a red bicycle. Chelsea assumed he was around ten years old. His face was flushed red. Another boy who looked younger was sitting on a blue bike nearby.

"Yes?" Chelsea said with a smile.

"Well, I think we are a little lost," he said, lowering his head. "My mom told me not to go too far, but we didn't listen. Do you have a phone? Could I call her to come by and pick us up?"

"Of course." She took out her cell from her jean pocket and looked at the screen, noticing a new text from her friend Neil. She quickly read it.

"In-laws making you go crazy yet?" it read. Chelsea rolled her eyes.

She gave the phone to the boy on the bicycle. "Here you go."

The boy looked up at her. "The screen's locked though."

Chelsea waved her hand at him. "There isn't a password. Just swipe to open it. Do you want me to show you how to call someone?"

The boy put the phone in his pocket. He turned his bike toward the road and jumped on the pedals. His friend on the blue bike was already starting to head off fast.

"Hey!" Chelsea yelled at the boy. "Stop!"

The boy on the red bicycle was laughing as he pedaled until Henry ran in front of him and knocked him off his bike. Henry quickly grabbed the boy and picked him up from the ground gently, but forcefully. Henry wiped dirt off the boy's clothes from the fall. He reached into the kid's pocket, grabbed the cell phone, and let go of the boy.

"Scram, kid," he said with a stern look. He watched as the boy picked up his bike and slowly started pedaling towards his friend on the road.

"Mike!" the boy yelled. "Wait for me!"

Henry looked back at Chelsea and slowly walked up to her; his hand stretched out with her phone. "I believe this is yours."

"I can't believe that happened," she said with a look of concern. "Those were, well, *bad boys*. Who does that?" She took her phone from his hand and opened it to make sure it wasn't broken. She was relieved when she saw it was fine.

Henry smiled. "When you move to Toronto, you better not be this gullible. That city will break you."

"Maybe we should call the cops?" Chelsea said, ignoring his comment.

"No, I lived in small towns my whole life. These boys are just *bored*. Thought you were an easy target."

"I'm not gullible!" she said. "The boy said he

was lost. He needed my phone. I didn't want him to end up... on a missing persons poster."

Henry smirked. "*Gullible*," he repeated. He looked down at the junk food on the ground. He bent over and picked up a smooshed brownie. "Now, this is a *tragedy*."

Chelsea waved her head. "I'm not going back inside that gas station to get another one! That old man inside is the worst, and so are those kids."

Henry grabbed her hand and kissed her wedding band. "Gullible and too sweet for your own good. If that old man was mean to you, you should tell him."

"He wasn't mean. He just... wasn't nice. I'm not that kind of girl to tell people what I think, you know that," Chelsea said, shoving him playfully. "That's why I married you."

Chapter Three

Chelsea finished the last of her snacks as Henry pulled onto a dirt road off the highway.

"About another twenty minutes," he said, taking a sip of his warm cola. He turned his head to look at Chelsea and with one hand sternly on the wheel, he brushed his hand against the side of her face.

Chelsea welcomed his touch, even though she hated the gritty feel of his sandpaper fingers. For someone who was very successful, he had the hands of a man who worked physical labor every day of his life.

Before being a successful business owner, Henry did have a hard life. From what he was willing to tell her about him growing up, she knew it was difficult. His father built the cabin in Kananaskis Country, int the middle of nowhere, moving his whole life into the woods, dragging Henry with him. Henry was forced to drop out of high school and was taught at home by his mother. He had no prom, no best friends, only his parents.

It wasn't until he was old enough to demand more from his life that his parents let him leave. Henry said when he was seventeen and set out to live his own life, it was almost as if he went into a different world when he left the woods.

It was also difficult to find work without

your high school diploma. He found stable work as a security guard and worked his way up to manager of the company within five years. Soon, an opportunity came to buy the company itself, and he took it. Now he owned and operated Secure Surveillance, one of the largest local security companies in the province.

Chelsea always admired that about him, his *drive*. He'd gone from being a jungle boy out in the woods to being head of the company and business owner, of it all within a handful of years.

Chelsea was twenty-one, and still figuring out life. She was a struggling painter, trying to have her paintbrush make a mark. When her friend Neil said he was going to go to a prestigious arts program at the University of Toronto, and asked her to join, she knew this was her opportunity, and like Henry she planned on taking it.

Henry didn't like it though.

The car started to slow as Henry rolled past a chain link fence. A large wood pole was cut in half, the other part face down in the grass below it. Soon they entered a wide, empty dirt parking lot.

Henry parked his truck. "We're here."

Chelsea smirked, waiting for him to say something that made sense. Instead, he turned off the ignition, and stepped out of the driver's seat. He stretched out his arms and moaned.

"What are you talking about Henry?" Chelsea shouted. "We're in the middle of nowhere."

Henry walked to the back of the truck, lowering the bed and taking out Chelsea's backpack. "I told you, that's where they live, in the middle of nowhere." He pointed towards a grouping of trees. "We have to go about four hours that way." He looked back at Chelsea with a smile, but she didn't return it. "What?" he said. "I'm not messing with you, it is!"

Chelsea sighed. "What did I sign up for?"

"A whole weekend of *fun*!" Henry answered with enthusiasm.

"It feels like it took a whole weekend to get here."

"And just four more hours to go." Henry handed her her backpack and Chelsea wrapped it around her shoulders. Henry put his on, and shut his truck bed, locking his vehicle with his fob key.

They walked for an hour into the woods. Chelsea tried to keep things lighthearted, but she was annoyed at Henry. Usually, when frustrated with someone, that person would never know that Chelsea felt hurt, but Henry was the only person to whom she was ever able to say what was on her mind. It was the reason she fell for him quickly. She felt safe with him. She could open up to him, about her life, everything she had gone through.

She lost her mother at a young age, and during the past year, her father as well from a heart attack. Henry was with her the whole time. He saw and understood her emotions, sometimes better than she did.

"Are you going to tell me?" he asked. Henry ducked under a low-lying tree branch and looked back at her. As Chelsea reached the branch, he lifted it for her until she was through. "You're upset? Is it because I dragged you out in the middle of nowhere to meet my parents?"

"No," Chelsea said, lowering her head. "You don't really think *poorly* of me, do you?"

"What do you mean?"

"*Gullible*? I mean, you don't think I'm *stupid*, right?"

Henry stopped walking and grabbed her hand softly. "No, I don't. I think the world of you. Gullible was... the wrong word to use. You're... just a good person. Some people try to take advantage of that."

Chelsea nodded. "Those boys could have needed help."

"I take it when you left the store, you didn't see the one on the red bicycle slip his cell phone in his other pocket?"

Chelsea furrowed her eyebrows. She didn't. How many people have those boys tricked? she thought to herself. She remembered the missing people on the board in the gas bar. "Well, that doesn't matter," she said. "Maybe their cell died, and they needed help. Sometimes people need help, and need good people, like me."

"You're right. Maybe I think too negatively

of people. I'm... sorry, okay?" He wrapped his hand around her waist and pulled Chelsea towards him, kissing her gently. "I mean it."

Chelsea smiled. "That's why I love you, Henry. You can admit to things. Please, don't ever change."

Chelsea held his hand tight. She remembered something her father told her, in his last few months while in the hospital recovering from another heart attack. "That man is special, Sea," he told her. Sea was a nickname he'd had for her for as long as she could remember. Her father had told Chelsea that her eyes were like her mother's and were as blue as the Atlantic. Her father didn't say it, but she knew he wanted to see her get married. She was his only child. She had dreamed of him walking her down the aisle, but with his deteriorating health, knew it wouldn't happen.

One night on a random date, Henry surprised her with a party at her favourite restaurant with friends and her father waiting. That night he proposed.

She covered her mouth in shock when Henry got down on one knee. Although they had only been together for six months, she was already head over heels for him. After he asked for her hand in marriage, Chelsea quickly looked at her father, who nodded in agreement. Soon after, her father's health began deteriorating further. Chelsea and

Henry initially planned to have their wedding at a church with a large party after, but none of that mattered to her anymore. Like every girl, Chelsea had dreamed about what her wedding day would be like, and she had big plans for it, but if her father wasn't there, it wouldn't have mattered.

Henry agreed to have the wedding within two months, and they were able to quickly get everything in order. Chelsea's father did walk her down the aisle. In the end she did have the wedding she wanted because the people she cared about most were with her.

Unfortunately, Henry's parents weren't able to attend. Chelsea hadn't even met her in-laws until this weekend. When Chelsea asked why they couldn't come, Henry rolled his eyes, telling her how particular they were. They hadn't left their cabin in the woods in years. Henry would bring anything they requested to them, if they needed anything, which was rare.

A month after the wedding, Chelsea's father passed.

Now it had been almost four months since he died. She grieved for her father but was starting to see the other side of her heartbreak.

Henry was with her the whole time, and she loved him even more for it. She felt bad for not being the newlywed wife he had dreamed of. Instead, she was a tearful mess. Now she was getting her life back on track, though. Now she wanted to go to art school in Toronto, and after, focus on her life with her husband, and maybe even a few kids along the way.

Chelsea got her foot stuck in some mud for a moment and twisted it out. She looked around at the dense woods surrounding them. How did Henry even know where to go? There was no discernable path. When she asked him, he said he knew these woods like the back of his hand. All she saw were trees and bushes, but they were like road signs to Henry.

"I thought you were used to camping as a kid?" he said.

"My father always took me," she said, "but nothing like this. We went to popular camps, and when he was older, we would rent RVs. Nothing off the grid, like you or your parents."

"Make sure to tell my parents that," he said. "The last girl I brought to them didn't know a lick about being out in the woods."

Chelsea laughed. "Here I was thinking I was the only girl you brought out in the middle of nowhere."

"Only a few I brought home to the parents," Henry said. He looked back at Chelsea and smiled. "They are going to love you."

Henry had said that a few times already on their trip. The more he said it, the more pressure she felt. What if they *hated* her?

She had assumed his parents were the type

to not want to be around people, given their chosen lifestyle. She had asked to meet them several times, but only now was Henry able to make it happen.

"I'm happy I finally get to meet them," she answered.

"It's the perfect weekend for it, too," Henry said. "I've got a huge project starting soon. It's going to be super busy. You have art school potentially starting in a week. Before all these hectic things happen, we get to spend some quality time with my folks."

Chelsea felt bitter when he said "*potentially*" going to art school. She wasn't sure what he hated more, the idea of her leaving the province or her going to school with Neil. They had talked/argued about it many times over the past month. Henry felt she was rushing into something, but Chelsea knew she was ready to start her life again. Neil wasn't a sexual threat to Henry. Since the first time they kissed, Chelsea only had eyes for her husband. With his looks and charm, it wasn't too hard to maintain. Neil, on the other hand, was just *Neil.* nothing more than a good friend.

Chelsea thought about saying something but didn't want to argue about it.

"Are we almost there?" she asked.

Henry nodded. "About an hour or so left."

"Ugh. I have to pee!"

Henry looked around the woods. "Pick your potty."

"An hour?" she repeated. "Fine!"

"What?" Henry laughed. "When you were in the Beavers when you were younger, you didn't go pee outside?"

"Beavers was for little boys. *Girl Guides* were for girls," she corrected.

Chelsea found a large tree and went out of sight from Henry. She pulled down her jeans and panties, and cautiously looked around before releasing. She hovered over a pile of leaves and felt a flick of urine on the side of her legs, making her wince. A sound of crunching leaves getting closer made her almost jump.

"Henry!" she yelled. "Can a girl get some privacy around here?"

The crunching sound stopped.

From a distance, Henry began shouting, "Eh Bear! Go Bear! Go!"

Chelsea froze. She heard movement from a bush near her, and the sound of something whizzing off into the woods.

Henry ran up to her. "Are you okay?"

"Was that a bear?" Chelsea managed to say between deep breaths.

"I'm not sure," Henry said. "It was something *big*. It's gone now."

"Oh boy!" Chelsea said, taking a deep breath.

"Didn't they teach you in Girl Guides that most of the animals out in the woods are more scared of you then you are of them?" He reached out his hand and Chelsea grabbed it. “Let's hurry up. We can get there soon.”

It took Chelsea some time to shrug off what happened, but when she found her pace again, they got to their destination. They soon made it to an area free of bushes and trees. She spotted the roof of a wood barn.

“Oh, thank god,” Chelsea exclaimed. Henry laughed.

A fence made with wood and nails surrounded a large clearing. They followed a dirt path that went to the gate. Henry lifted the latch to open it, and Chelsea noticed a large sign tacked to the fence that read “Do Not Trespass” and another below it that read “Property Under Video Surveillance.”

They walked down the path that led to a large one-storey cabin. Chelsea's father would have loved a place like this. He would have enjoyed booking a vacation at a cabin in the woods. She couldn't imagine living here year-round, though.

“You should see the large garden in the back,” Henry said. ‘I'm sure my parents will show you. They're so proud of it.”

Chelsea did enjoy gardening. She'd had a small tomato plant at their apartment in Calgary but somehow killed it within a few days.

Henry walked up the wood stairs to the front door, with Chelsea taking her time behind him. He knocked and waited.

Chelsea noticed a camera on the porch facing them. Henry answered her before she could ask.

"Runs on a generator," he said. "I installed their whole system. It's amazing what you can do now."

Chelsea nodded and waited anxiously for the door to open. She heard no movement from inside the home. She peeked inside a window and saw three fabric chairs sitting beside a metal fireplace. There were no lights on inside, or movement.

Henry knocked on the door again, harder. "Mom! Dad!" he yelled. After another minute of waiting, he looked at Chelsea. "I guess they're not home. Maybe we should go back to the truck and come back a different time?" When Chelsea didn't react to his joke, he laughed to himself. "They could be in the garden." Henry waved at Chelsea to follow him down the porch steps, but then she heard a creak at the front door.

It slowly opened, and a woman dressed in a black dress to her knees stepped out. Henry has told her she was in her early fifties but could easily have passed for a woman in her forties. Her thick, dark eyebrows raised when she saw Henry.

"Henry!" She wrapped her arms around him tight. "Please, come inside. Your father and I have been waiting all day!" She forcefully grabbed him and guided him inside.

Henry shouted, "Dad!"

Chelsea smiled to herself, taking in the moment of seeing Henry reunite with his family.

His mother noticed her. Immediately her face, once bright with happiness, slumped to a more neutral demeanour.

"You must be Chelsea," she said to her daughter-in-law. Before Chelsea could answer, Henry's mother turned from her and gestured for her to follow. "Come inside!" she yelled to Chelsea.